The Two Jays Adventure

The Two Jays Adventure
by
Chris Wright

ISBN: 978-1-5203448-8-1

Also available as an e-Book ISBN: 978-0-9954549-8-9

Website: www.whitetreepublishing.com
More books by Chris Wright on
www.rocky-island.com
Email: wtpbristol@gmail.com

The Two Jays Adventure is a work of fiction. Names, characters, places, and incidents are the product of the author's imagination or are used fictitiously.

(See also www.youversion.com for free downloads of over a thousand Bible translations in over a thousand languages on your phone, tablet, and computer.)

Published by
White Tree Publishing
Bristol
UNITED KINGDOM

A Word from the Author

I first wrote this story some years ago, and things have now changed a lot, especially with electronics and digital communication. No mobile (cell) phones, digital cameras, tablets and computers back then. So although the main story is unchanged, some things have been updated to make the adventure happen today.

Note that in America a mother is a mom, while over on the Two Jays' side of the Atlantic a mother is a mum. Fathers are usually known as dad on both sides. English trainers are what Americans call sneakers, a tap is called a faucet in America, and a cupboard is called a closet. Pyjamas are pajamas in America. I'm sure you get the general idea. There are a few other differences, especially in the way some words are spelt. This book uses the British English words and spelling because that's where the adventure takes place.

Chris Wright

Measurements

The measurements in this book are in miles, feet and inches. Here is an approximate table of conversion to metric.

1 mile is 1.6km

1 yard is a little less than 1m

1 foot is 30cm

I hope this helps!

Chapters

Chapter One

THE FIRST DISCOVERY

"When I'm on holiday, I like adventures," Jessica Green said, with a long sigh.

Her cousin James stared at the peaceful Mendip hills rising high above them.

"We seem to be in the middle of nowhere," Jessica continued. "It's so quiet. I can't think much ever happens here."

She was mistaken. Very mistaken. A shout from the other side of the valley made them jump.

"What was that?" Jessica asked, standing astride two mounds of grass. As she turned to look, there came another shout followed by a laugh. "Can you see who it is, James?"

James shook his head. "I haven't the faintest idea. I can't see anyone. Yes I can. There, on that rock. Two of them. A boy ... and another one, older than us."

"Let's go over and see what they want," Jessica suggested.

James held back. "I'm not sure. The older one's holding a catapult."

"So what?"

James stared at the two boys. "I don't know, but——"

"Oh, come on!"

"Yes, all right."

Jessica, her long, blonde hair blowing in the gentle breeze, looked ahead. "We can't go this way in any case. There's a stream running everywhere. We'll *have* to go across."

Suddenly James felt silly. Of course there was nothing to be afraid of. The older boy, a youth really, wouldn't use the catapult on them ... would he?

As they crossed the valley, picking their way carefully through the marshy patches, James paused. They were now close enough to hear what was being shouted. Various insults such as, "Don't get your baby feet wet!" and "Where are your skipping ropes?" This one came as they jumped from one piece of dry ground to the next. The younger boy kept laughing all the time. There was no point in avoiding them now.

The older of the two had long, greasy hair. James decided there was something rather unpleasant about him.

"What are you doing here?" the owner of the catapult demanded.

James noticed the way the younger boy kept looking at his companion in admiration.

“Is this the way to Saint Cerig’s well?” James asked.

“Might be,” the older of the two muttered, taking a half-smoked cigarette from his pocket. “Might not be.”

“In which case, thank you!” Jessica said in disgust.

The youth took the unlit cigarette from his mouth. “Now hold on a minute.” He fingered his catapult. “Just don’t be in a hurry. This is my patch here, see. Just for shooting. You’d be surprised at some of the things I shoot.”

“And people,” the younger boy added with a giggle. This was the first time he’d spoken to them. They both had strong West Country accents.

“You shut up, nipper. Who spoke to you? Now then, I wouldn’t want to be using this.” The youth pulled back the heavy elastic of his catapult. “I think you’d better both be off – and don’t come round here again.” With this he put the cigarette back in his mouth, and lit it.

In silence they stared at each other. The youth half closed his eye in what was obviously meant to be a threatening manner, although the effect was probably not as startling as he hoped. He let his mouth turn up into a sneer. As he took a long draw on his cigarette, he gave a loud cough which blew the cigarette from between his fingers. With watering eyes he groped for it on the wet ground.

When he found it, it was damp, rather muddy and had gone out.

James and Jessica resumed their walk down the valley. When they were at least a hundred yards away, Jessica said, “I think he’s stupid.”

James was sure he could feel the two of them staring at him. “I don’t trust him. The young one’s all right. He’s just a hanger-on. But the other one’s——”

There was a twang of high-powered elastic. James and Jessica fell flat on their faces as a stone tore through the branches of a nearby tree. The laughter that followed made them realise that this had only been done to frighten them.

“Don’t turn round,” James warned. “Just keep walking. They wouldn’t dare try to hit us. All the same, I hope we don’t keep bumping into them.”

Jessica shook her head in bewilderment. “It’s fantastic. We come to a lonely place like this, and when we *do* meet someone, it has to be *them*!”

“I’m going to call them the Ghastly Pair,” James decided, taking an extra long jump, missing the next dry patch and getting a trainer full of water. “Don’t worry, we may never see them again.”

James Cooper and Jessica Green, the Two Jays for short, were just starting a family holiday at Sheppingford. Jessica was James’s cousin, and they lived close to each other at home. A man who worked with James’s father had recommended a very cheap holiday cottage at the foot of the Mendip hills in Somerset. His recommendations had been so glowing that soon after Christmas James's father had booked a fortnight for the second half of August.

There had been nearly eight months for looking forward to it, but the time had arrived at last. For James, a holiday like this would have been unthinkable without Jessica for company, so it had been taken for granted that Jessica would be coming.

"I'm always glad when Jessica's around," James's mother had said. "It keeps you both nicely out of the way." James would have been pleased with this observation if his mother hadn't added, "If not out of trouble!"

They began to climb to higher and drier ground, and came to an old track that led into a small quarry that looked deserted. A man was pushing his bicycle towards them. When he saw them he shouted angrily.

"I don't think he wants us to go any closer," James muttered. "Come on, it won't be here, anyway. My dad would have known if Saint Cerig's well was in a quarry."

Jessica Green nodded. "I can't see why an old quarry like this should be private, but...." She glanced back at the man again. "Yes, I think we'd better go. Of course, you could try asking him...."

James Cooper laughed. "No, we'll go on looking by ourselves. Saint Cerig's well. Dad said it would be hard to find. And he said it won't be like Jack and Jill's well, with a bucket on the end of a rope. It will be a small hole in the ground with flat stones around it to stand on. The water in it might be bubbling up, or it might be still."

"Don't be disappointed," Jessica warned. "I can't think there's going to be much of a mystery in Saint Cerig's well if it's just a small hole in the ground. I was hoping there might be treasure at the bottom!"

James stood in the lane below the quarry, the angry man with the bicycle temporarily forgotten. When they'd arrived earlier that day with his parents, he and Jessica had wanted to get straight out and explore. No, they didn't want to sit down and rest after the long car journey. They just wanted to see what was out there.

James's father had sent them to find the old holy well, known as Saint Cerig's well, which was supposed to have been a cure for all ills. Whether it had ever really worked, he said he had no idea, but he thought a search for it might work wonders for a pair of impatient holidaymakers.

James had a pocket compass combined with a magnifying glass. They'd used the compass part of it a couple of times to get their bearings. The last thing they wanted to do was to get lost — in hostile territory!

The Mendips were high but hazy in the late afternoon light. Nearby they could see some much smaller hills. Then they spotted a few trees around what might once have been another, much smaller quarry. It was unlikely they would be chased away from this one. So, little suspecting what they were about to find, they crossed the lane and made their way through the undergrowth.

"I think we've found the well," Jessica called loudly, for James was a little way behind. "If you come here—— Oh!" She stepped back and her face went pale.

James pushed forward. "What's the matter? Is...? It's ... it's not dead, is it?"

The sheepdog was curled up on the wet earth, beside a deep pool near the rock face. James looked up at the rock. The lower part looked as though it had been smoothed away at some time, leaving a miniature cliff perhaps twice his own height. Not high enough, surely, to have killed this dog – even if it had been careless enough to fall over.

It was still breathing, but panting as though in great distress. Maybe it had been shot – with a catapult. Jessica tried to see if it had a nametag on its collar, but the dog growled unpleasantly as she put her hand near.

"Dad will know what to do," James said. "Let's go and tell him."

Somehow the sight of the dog had put an end to the expedition. The way back was easy to find, and when he saw the holiday cottage again, James started to feel much better. He pushed open the brown-painted front gate. Yes, it was going to be good at Sheppingford. The cottage was fantastic. The slate roof, the small windows, the ivy growing everywhere. This was his first chance to inspect the cottage properly. There were a few flowers growing in the garden, but he had no idea what they were. Perhaps Jessica would know.

The cottage was empty. His parents must have gone out for a bit of exploring on their own. The front room smelt slightly old and damp. There was a brass oil lamp on the table. It would be fun to try to get it working one night. He glanced up at the ceiling and saw a single low power bulb that looked almost as old as the cottage. In that case, they would probably need the oil lamp as well!

Jessica laughed when James told her what he was thinking. “It’s a bit sort of olden-days,” she agreed. “Come and see the kitchen!”

Jessica showed her cousin the old kitchen range. It was like something from a Victorian picture-book. A large closed-in fireplace with black cast-iron ovens at each side.

“That!” exclaimed James. “What does it burn? Lumps of peat?”

“I don’t think we’ll be needing to light it,”

Jessica said. "There's not much to cook with, though. Just a microwave. And it's a really ancient microwave. Oh look, there's a gas hob with just two small burners. Mum and Dad aren't going to like it."

By the time they'd inspected the outside sanitary arrangements, James was starting to wonder whether his parents hadn't gone for a walk, but had taken the car and gone for good!

Going to the front gate they could hear voices coming from further down the lane. They decided to investigate and found James's parents returning from a stroll to post a letter. The Two Jays told their story of the dog, but said nothing about the older boy with the catapult. James knew his mother would worry.

"You'd best report it to one of the farms," James's father advised. "I'll come with you if you like. We ought to go immediately. Was there a name on the collar?"

"We ... we didn't like to touch it," James confessed. "The dog didn't like us."

His father nodded. "Best not to risk it in the circumstances."

Mrs. Cooper said she was going to stay behind to pick flowers, and then have a go at putting everything away tidily in the cottage. From the way she was talking, James wasn't sure whether his mother was happy about the place, or not.

"The, er ... cottage," his father said quietly. "I heard about it through a friend at work. Don't tell your mother this, James, but it's much more primitive than I was led to believe."

"It's fun though," Jessica said.

"What's fun?" Mrs. Cooper called, reaching for some red flowers high up in the hedge that surrounded the cottage.

"The cottage, Mum," James said, surprised that his mother had been able to hear.

"Oh yes, I'm sure you two are going to find it fun. I'm not so sure what to think of it myself. I think it's much more primitive than your father was led to believe!"

"Honestly, Mum. Fancy you hearing what Dad said!"

Mrs. Cooper merely raised her eyebrows and gave a small shrug, pretending not to understand. James smiled to himself. He knew his parents loved each other, and he loved them.

It wasn't far to the nearest farm. The farmer looked serious and went with the three of them to see the dog. Yes, it was his. He bent down to examine it closely. The dog gave a whimper and wagged its tail slightly.

"Been poisoned," the farmer grunted.

"Poisoned?" James asked, glancing over his shoulder for the youth with the catapult. "Do you think it could've been sort of ... shot?"

The farmer picked the large sheepdog up in his arms. James thought he could see anger as well as sadness in the man's eyes. "No, not shot. Definitely poisoned. Like my sheep."

Chapter Two

TWO STONE HEADS

"Come on, you lazy lumps," James's father called out the next morning. "Don't forget it's Sunday today. The service starts at ten o'clock here, not eleven."

The Two Jays had seen the small country church the day before, and were interested in going to the service in what was a much older building than their church back home. At ten to ten the family made their way up the uneven, well-worn steps of the ancient building. The dark blue notice board announcing the times of the services had recently been repainted with gold lettering.

Inside, a young woman was playing hymn tunes on the small organ. There were only a handful of people there. Quietly the family leaned forward to pray. Until recently, James had often wondered what people prayed about before the service. He'd heard of people who knelt down and counted slowly to a hundred before getting up, in order to appear to be holy. But for eight weeks now he'd felt this was unlikely to be the right thing to do.

Jessica knew. There were so many things to pray about. She prayed for the Holy Spirit to come, and for the minister, that God would speak through him. For everyone who was going to be at the service – and there weren't very many yet, she noticed. And then for herself, that she might not only learn something, but be able to praise God well.

She sat back in the ancient pew. James sat back too, and smiled at her. It had taken him slightly longer than counting to a hundred, but he'd also made good use of the time.

As ten o'clock drew near, people arrived in a rush, and soon most of the pews were occupied. Perhaps the country people were busy, and not able to get there any earlier. Whatever the reason, they seemed to be a happy lot. They smiled and nodded to their visitors, and James felt quite embarrassed to be the centre of so much attention.

The minister was a young man. James decided he'd like to meet him afterwards. He seemed such a normal sort of person. Which of course, James reflected, is what a minister should be. All those Bible people the minister was talking about, like Ezekiel and Isaiah, might have been quite normal as well, but sometimes it was difficult to think so when you saw them on stained glass windows or in old engravings. But the way this minister talked about them made you think you'd really met them.

James listened hard, but occasionally his eyes wanted to look around the church.

Embedded in the high pulpit he noticed two very small human heads, carved from stone. They stared down at the congregation in a rather disturbing way. One looked down to the left, and the other down to the right. Indeed, a small, mediaeval painting directly on the plaster of the wall showed a strange, bearded figure standing with a book in his hands. The painting looked as old as the church. Who could it be?

A final hymn and the service was over, with the villagers greeting each other as they began to shuffle out. James and Jessica decided to give the building a closer inspection.

Suddenly Jessica grabbed hold of James's arm. "That man, just going out! He's the one who wouldn't let us near that old quarry!"

James turned round to see the man leaving the church. He must have been sitting at the back. The minister shook hands with him as though he came every week. The man caught sight of the Two Jays, smiled at them, and then walked down the church steps. He seemed friendly enough, so why had he shouted at them so angrily to keep away from the quarry?

"I've heard about you," the minister said, walking over to the Two Jays. "We like to get to know our visitors. You're staying at the old cottage, aren't you?"

Jessica laughed. "Old? It must be the oldest thing around. Have you ever been inside?"

"Ah well," the minister replied, "I dare say it is a bit old – and a bit damp at times – but most people seem to enjoy staying in it, after a few days."

"I think it's great," James put in quickly. "It's the best place I've ever stayed in. Except there's no telly and no internet, so we can't watch anything. There's no phone signal indoors either, but we can go in the garden and go online okay. So yes, I really like it here."

The minister laughed at James's enthusiasm. "Now then, I don't know your names yet."

"I'm James Cooper."

"And I'm Jessica Green. I'm James's cousin."

"My name's Peterson. John Peterson."

"We guessed that was you," James said. He pointed to the notice board. "We saw your name there."

"It's ever such an interesting church," Jessica added.

James's father came over and introduced himself to the minister. Then he turned to James. "You and Jessica can stay and have a look round here, if you like. I'll walk back with your mother. She's rather anxious to see how to cook Sunday lunch with just a microwave and two gas rings. So don't expect anything too special!"

James wanted a closer look at the old wall painting he'd noticed during the service.

James pointed up. "That man? Is he Saint Cerig? He's supposed to have a holy well near here somewhere, isn't he?"

John Peterson nodded. "Not only a well, but a small house. Some think it might have been a chapel. That's part of it in the picture. The painting was hidden behind white paint, and it was uncovered twenty years ago when the church was being redecorated. Saint Cerig lived here nearly seven hundred years ago. There's not a trace of any building now. All we have left is his well in the middle of a field."

"Middle of a *field}*" James asked in surprise. "Surely——"

But the minister had gone for a moment, to collect his books.

The Two Jays examined the painting again. The colours were mostly brown and it was obviously ancient. There was certainly a stone wall by the side of the saint. Saint? He was a funny-looking man. A limerick ran through James's head.

There was an old man with a beard,
Who said, "It is just as I feared.
"Two owls and a hen,
"Four larks and a wren,
"Have all built their nests in my beard."

The minister came out of the vestry.

"It's a great painting," James said. "Is it ever so old?"

"It's believed to be late fifteenth century."

James looked up again and thought hard. "Over five hundred years old!" Then, "That's really old," he added in the quiet tone he usually used in churches, empty or full. "I think it's ever so interesting."

"My wife will be here soon. She might be able to tell you more," Mr. Peterson said. "She runs a Discoverers group for the younger children during the prayers and talk."

James had noticed several children go out during the second hymn, and the mystery was solved. But not the mystery of Saint Cerig's well. The small well they'd found was definitely *not* in the middle of a field!

At that moment the door of the church hall burst open, and a dozen children ran out. A woman followed them, and the minister introduced her to James and Jessica as his wife. No, she knew very little about the wall painting — or Saint Cerig. His well was the only thing anyone knew about him. Apart from that — perhaps they could try and find out something for themselves.

As they moved off, the Two Jays noticed that most of the children from Discoverers were being met by their parents who'd been at church themselves. One member was being met by someone the Two Jays had encountered before. Together, they were known to James and Jessica as the Ghastly Pair!

So far they hadn't noticed the Two Jays. "When *are* you going to give it up, little 'un?" the older boy asked. His hair was slightly less greasy today. Perhaps it had been cleaned in preparation for Sunday. Not that it looked as though Sunday meant much to him. Even so, perhaps he regarded it as an opportunity for a clean-up.

"My mum says I shan't be going much more," the younger boy told him.

"That's right, little 'un. No point in being indoors today. Coming out now?"

The boy said he had to have his lunch first, but he could go out in the afternoon.

"Right then, see you at two!" the older one said. Then he noticed James and Jessica. "Why, it's you!" he said scornfully in his strong Somerset accent. "I suppose you've been to church! Huh!"

"Huh! yourself," Jessica retorted, sticking out her tongue in as rude a way as she could manage.

The youth looked a bit taken aback by this. Unable to think of anything further to say, he went "Huh!" once more and walked quickly down the road, his hands thrust deep into the pockets of his jeans.

"I'm not sure sticking your tongue out was a

good witness to your faith," James said, "but he definitely deserved it. I expect Mr. Peterson would know who he is. Ministers seem to know that sort of thing."

<><><>

They got the chance to ask later in the day. After an early tea James and Jessica set off for a walk on their own. In the village they met the minister and his wife, also having a stroll before the evening service. They talked for a while, and then James mentioned the two boys they'd met.

"They're horrible," Jessica said. "Who are they?"

The minister frowned. "The older one is Greg Hawker. I'm concerned about him. He's a bad influence on young Brian Tucker."

"Is Brian Tucker the young one who hangs around with Greg?" James asked.

"That's right. They live next door to each other down near the main road."

Mrs. Peterson was picking tall grasses. "I feel sorry for Brian," she said thoughtfully. "That Hawker boy is a bit of a bully. I'm afraid he's going to get into trouble with that catapult of his."

"Oh come, now," Mr. Peterson reproved. "He's hardly a gangster. A bit inclined to show off, but not the violent type."

"Can't anyone stop him?" Jessica asked. "Somehow I can't imagine James being allowed to go around like that!"

Mr. Peterson thought for a moment, then he said, "Greg's father thinks his boy is big and tough, which of course he is — in a way. Brian's father left home a few years ago. His mother thinks he needs a man for company, and Greg is the next best thing."

James said nothing. He couldn't understand anyone wanting Greg Hawker for company.

"Brian's a nice enough boy," Mrs. Peterson said. "He's in our Discoverers."

"That's why my wife's got a soft spot for him," Mr. Peterson explained, with a wink.

Mrs. Peterson smiled and gathered her grasses into a neat bundle. "Take no notice of my husband," she said. "He's just as concerned as I am about Brian — and about Greg. I'm afraid Brian may soon leave our Discoverers. Greg keeps trying to get him to stop coming."

James was helping Jessica pick some of the long grasses now. A large bunch of grasses would look good in the cottage. "I don't like Greg," he said, from the top of a high bank. "I can't imagine *he* ever went to Discoverers."

Mrs. Peterson helped James climb down. "You'd be surprised. Greg came every week until a couple of years ago. Then all of a sudden he stopped, and now he seems to be against our church and all it stands for."

James climbed the opposite bank, grabbed at

some more grasses, and raced down into the road. Fortunately no traffic was coming. "There was a man in church," he said suddenly.

"Oh yes," Jessica explained. "The man who works at that old quarry up the hill."

"I know who you mean," Mr. Peterson said. "Mr. Slade. He comes along to church most Sundays."

"It's just that.... Oh well, never mind," James said.

The minister raised his eyebrows, obviously expecting to hear more.

"Well," James went on, "we were exploring yesterday and he started shouting and yelling at us."

Mr. Peterson laughed. "I expect you went near the quarry."

"Only a bit," James said. "Anyway, what's so special about the place?"

"It doesn't do to go upsetting our Mr. Slade." Once again the minister laughed. "He's a nice enough person really."

"Nice?" Jessica asked. "Are you sure?"

"Yes, quite sure. He's the local stonemason. Cuts his own stone there, and is afraid other people will take it. Most people keep away, although it isn't *his* quarry anyway. Anyone in the village is entitled to use it if they need stone, but no one bothers. Mr. Slade makes all sorts of shaped stone for building.

That quarry was part of an old lead mine once."

"Mine?" James asked. "That sounds exciting."

"Old mines can be very dangerous," Mr. Peterson warned.

As James and Jessica assured him they'd be careful, Mr. Peterson stopped by a high stone wall outside an old house. "There's only the one mineshaft, and it's nearly filled in, right up to the top. By the way, did you hear about the poisoned animals?"

James suddenly felt frightened. "We found a sick sheepdog yesterday. The farmer said something about his sheep being poisoned. Is that right?"

Mr. Peterson nodded. "I'm afraid so. Two weeks ago there were two dead sheep by the pond in a lower field. There's a little well in the field. It looks to me as though they're getting poisoned through the water, but the Environment Agency is blaming Mr. Osborne, the farmer."

James had felt upset by the sheepdog. He couldn't bear the thought of any animals dying in that field. If the dog had been poisoned through the water, he might be in danger himself — and Jessica, and his parents. "How do you mean, through the water?" he asked, dreading the answer.

Mrs. Peterson set his mind at rest. "Not the tap water. That comes from a reservoir near Cheddar. The water at these springs comes from the ditches and streams on the hills around here."

The minister looked up at the Two Jays. "You must be very careful if you go near the wells and streams. Don't drink any water unless it's from a proper tap." He looked at his watch. "Oh dear, we've been talking too long. I like to be indoors and have some peace and quiet before the service. It starts at six. See you there."

At his home church, James often went to both the morning and evening services. Once a month there was a special get-together at someone's house for all the young people who'd been at the evening service. He doubted whether anything like that ever happened at Sheppingford, but he was looking forward to hearing Mr. Peterson again.

James's parents, who went along to church with him at home, met the Two Jays at the church door. The service was bright and lively. It must have been interesting, because James thought no more about Saint Cerig – or his well.

Outside, they said goodbye to the minister and his wife. James's parents were going straight back to the cottage, but the James and Jessica decided to do a bit of exploring while it was still light. There were so many places to see, interesting things to discover, and only two weeks for doing it!

They took their time and added more grasses to Jessica's collection. About halfway back, the lane ran through a small wood with high banks on either side. As they rounded the corner, there, standing in the middle of the road, was the older of the Ghastly Pair — complete with catapult.

"Been to church I suppose," he said, flicking his hair back with a nod of his head.

James and Jessica stood firm.

The youth, now known as Greg Hawker, started walking towards them slowly. "You keep away from that church," he threatened.

"We won't be going much more," Jessica said mischievously. Greg looked pleased, until she added, "We're only here for one more Sunday!"

"What's wrong with church?" James asked.

Greg was now close. Had he really been going to church until two years ago? It was difficult to believe it.

"Wrong with church? Huh! You keep away from it. Religion!" Greg spat on the ground, but it wasn't a very good spit, so he tried again. This time with even less success. "Religion? It's soft! And they're trying to make everyone else go soft, too. I had enough of it when I was younger."

James decided it was no good trying to explain that some of the people in the Bible were amongst the bravest and toughest in history. Although Greg Hawker probably wouldn't be able to see it, it was possible to mix bravery with being a Christian. In fact, it was often necessary!

Wham! A flying lump of earth caught James on

the back of his neck. Brian Tucker had crept up behind them, and was now preparing to throw another lump. Really, he thought, the Ghastly Pair were absolutely, absolutely ... ghastly!

James could feel the earth trickling slowly down the inside of his shirt. He wouldn't fight back. Jessica wouldn't welcome a fight. In any case it was Sunday – not a day for fighting. A surprised Greg Hawker let them pass unharmed.

Chapter Three

THE KITE

That evening, with the yellow light from the brass oil lamp adding to the feeble glow from the single bulb in the middle of the ceiling, the family was reading. James had a magazine with a section on early flying.

"This is fantastic!" he said suddenly, making everyone jump.

Jessica pushed her book away. "This isn't very good. What's fantastic?"

"It says here that during the First World War the soldiers used to spy on the enemy lines by sending up a man in a basket hanging from a balloon."

"How did he get back?"

"They pulled him down again."

"Oh, the balloon was tied to the ground?"

"Yes, of course. You didn't think.... Oh, Jessica!"

"Well, what's fantastic about that, then?" Jessica demanded.

"That bit isn't, but just listen to this. They also sent men up hanging from a kite."

"A kite?" Much to James's relief, Jessica was

sounding quite interested, but his parents had gone back to their reading.

"There's a picture here. It's a sort of box kite. The man under it has an old fashioned camera, probably to photograph the enemy lines. Let's make a kite."

"Have we got enough stuff? We'd need cloth and sticks, and some strong cord. The wind can be ever so strong. Do you know what to do?"

"Do?" James now wondered if he'd been just a bit too sure of himself. "I've not made one since ages ago," he admitted, "but I 'spect it's like swimming and riding a bike. You sort of never forget."

Jessica closed her book firmly. "A box kite. They're supposed to fly well, aren't they?"

"They must do, if people flew hanging underneath them with a camera. We'll make one and you can be first up!"

"Thanks," Jessica said with a shudder. "It was your idea."

"Was it? That's okay, I'll be needed on the ground to control it. Let's start on it first thing in the morning."

Jessica was impatient. "No, now. There's probably enough stuff around here to get started. Let's look."

They did look but there was nothing. James said they might have to buy what they needed.

"We'll get it in Wells or Glastonbury first thing tomorrow," he said, sitting down again. "Dad can take us there in the car. Let's make a list of the things we need. Cloth. String. Some bamboos for the frame."

Mrs. Cooper looked up from her book. "Did you say you're going to make a kite?"

The Two Jays nodded.

"I might be able to help. I'll see, when you've gone up to bed. I brought one or two extra sheets. One of them is torn down one side. I was going to mend it over the holidays, but I don't suppose I'll ever get round to it."

Jessica smiled. She liked James's mum, her Aunty Amy. That sheet would never be mended! The Cooper family had hundreds of things that were going to be fixed when they got round to them. But they were all so happy that it would surely be a sad day if all the jobs were done.

Ever since she could remember, life had been like that in the Cooper household. Aunty Amy, Uncle Clive and James were all the same. Her mum and Aunty Amy were sisters, but they were so different. Her own mum was part of the "Let's do it now" brigade, and Aunty Amy was part of the "Let's leave it till tomorrow" set.

Jessica knew she was always impatient. Always wanting to get on with things. She liked to think she was having a good influence on James, because there were times when he also wanted to get on with things.

James clapped his hands with joy. “A sheet, Mum? Can you look for it now?”

“When you’ve gone to bed. The morning will be quite soon enough. And by the way, talking about bed....”

James groaned and knew what was coming next. There were only two proper bedrooms. His parents had one and Jessica had the other. James had a folding bed in what was really little more than a cupboard on the landing. All the same, James thought it was just about okay, as long as the door onto the landing was left slightly open.

James thought back to what had happened eight weeks ago. He’d been given a modern translation of the Bible for his birthday. An uncle he hardly knew had sent it to him. James had read bits of it, and somehow hadn’t been able to put it down.

It was while reading it one evening he had made his great discovery. He still read from it every day. After eight weeks it was becoming quite a habit. He knew Jessica read regularly from her own Bible before getting up in the morning. It was always by the side of her bed, even on holiday.

After reading a few verses, James leaned forward and prayed to God, his heavenly Father. Some people would have called it “saying prayers,” but James knew there was a big difference between praying and "saying prayers."

And so their first complete day came to an end. James, feeing excited about the kite, stayed awake in his "cupboard" and planned exactly how they would make it from the old sheet.

<><><>

Jessica was dragging him out of bed early the next morning – before he'd finished his planning, it seemed.

"I'm going for a walk up the hill," Jessica announced. Then as James tried to climb back under the blanket, she added. "And you're coming too."

It was no good protesting. Jessica always meant what she said. Anyway, it looked a nice sunny morning. Yes, he *would* go. It was a great idea. Why hadn't he thought of it? Because he'd been asleep. Yes.... Oh well, better get dressed.

The grass was wet underfoot. Some of the water came from tiny springs deep under the ground. There had been a heavy dew. It was a morning to be prepared with wellington boots. Silvery drops of water stood out on every blade of grass. The sun, hidden by their own hill, shone golden yellow on the high Mendips.

They climbed to the top of a small hill with a wide view of the surrounding countryside. On their way back to the cottage for breakfast they met the farmer who'd gone with them to the well. Mr.

Osborne — or Farmer Osborne — James remembered he was called.

"How's the dog?" Jessica asked. "He looked ever so poorly on Saturday."

"Fair to middling," Farmer Osborne said. "It's a real mystery how them's getting the poison. Did you hear about them other animals?"

"Two of your sheep died a couple of weeks ago, didn't they?" Jessica asked.

The farmer nodded glumly. "It were worse two months ago. I near lost a horse through it. The vet said it had been poisoned by brushwood killer. The Environment Agency sent an inspector along, and took a sample from the well where you found my dog, and all the other springs and wells roundabouts. The report came back that everything were clear. He searched around my farm and found some sealed containers of brushwood killer. I were going to use it to clear the end of the bottom field, but I never got round to it."

"Then how could it have been you?" James asked in surprise. "Not if you haven't used it."

"Well," Farmer Osborne said, "he didn't say it in so many words, but he reckoned I'd tipped an outdated container into the well. The water is often almost stagnant there, and takes a long time to clear, unless we've had heavy rain. No other animals have access to my land, so he said it must have been my fault anyhow."

James looked up at the sturdy Somerset farmer. It was strange that it had all happened before, and in the field where they'd found the dog by the well. Perhaps they could do something, on their own of course. Yes, it would be worth having a good look at the wells and springs all around here and come up with some clues.

James decided not to say anything. They would have to make another visit to the well where they found the dog. Perhaps it wasn't Saint Cerig's well anyway!

The kite-making came to nothing. Mrs. Cooper had "forgotten" to bring a needle and thread, and as it turned out she'd even forgotten to bring the torn sheet. Jessica thought it was just too convenient, and typical of James's family.

So a trip into nearby Wells was called for. James's mother wanted to do some shopping anyway, and Jessica hoped to get a couple of books she'd been wanting to read for some time.

Jessica was amazed to hear Wells being called a city, and not only a city, but the smallest city in England. James's father explained it was a city because it had a cathedral. Not only did it have a cathedral, but it had a shop that sold a variety of kites. James insisted that the large red, green and blue model was exactly what *he* wanted, Jessica found one of the books *she* wanted, and his mother also found things *she* wanted. James's father seemed quite happy to go and have a cup of coffee and read the paper.

<><><>

"Is it ready?" Jessica asked impatiently, as James insisted he knew exactly how to assemble the kite as soon as they returned to the cottage.

"Let's find out," James said. "If we can't get it to fly, then it isn't! Come on, we'll try it right now."

They chose the hill behind the cottage for the first flight. Fern Hill, it was known as locally. Below the trees at the top was a fairly clear patch. Jessica laid the kite on the ground, and James walked into the gusty wind, unrolling the twin lines until he was more than thirty yards away. Jessica held the kite in the air, and James began to run with the lines.

To their relief the kite became airborne at once. James let some of the twin lines run out and the kite climbed rapidly. It looked impressive. He began to let out some more line. Suddenly the kite swooped alarmingly towards Jessica. Then it climbed steeply and swooped down again. Jessica hurried to join her cousin.

"I don't think it likes me!" she said breathlessly.

"Well don't come here," James protested. "It might attack me by mistake! Something does seem a bit wrong. I think I let the lines out too fast. Here, you take over."

Jessica tried, and by letting the twin lines out

slowly and evenly, the kite climbed majestically overhead.

The late afternoon sun shone brightly on the fields below. The drainage ditches running round the flat fields in the valley shone like silver pathways. On lower ground, and close to them, was the small rock face where they'd found Farmer Osborne's sheepdog. And there yes, it must be – the little pool of water they thought was Saint Cerig's well. Or was it? Hadn't Mr. Peterson, the minister, said the well was in the *middle* of a field?

As they looked, James had a horrible feeling they were being watched. Slowly he turned to look behind. Greg Hawker and his admiring companion were creeping up the hill towards them.

James wasn't sure what to do now. They'd probably seen the kite flying and were coming to make trouble. It was unlikely they'd come to watch. Greg Hawker held out his catapult, took aim at the kite, and let fly with a small stone.

"He's missed," Jessica said.

"I don't think it will do any harm if he hits it," James said quietly. "The fabric's too soft to be damaged." Then he added, "I hope!"

The Ghastly Pair were closer now. Greg Hawker fired several more stones but they all either missed or had no effect. The Two Jays stood their ground.

"Don't pull it in," Jessica warned, "or they'll think they've won."

"You're right," James agreed. "But I know what we *can* do."

The opposition were now directly under the kite. James pulled on one of the lines. It was supposed to be a stunt kite, but he'd not yet got used to doing anything more than trying to keep it in the air. Down and down it swooped, straight for the ground and the Ghastly Pair! Greg Hawker ran to one side, and Brian Tucker fell flat on his face shouting, "You've hit 'im! You've shot 'im down!"

James pulled on the other line and the kite began climbing steadily again.

Brian Tucker picked himself up and seemed to be looking on the ground for the wreckage, while the kite soared high above him. Greg Hawker took another shot with his catapult. Once again James made the kite dive at the ground.

"Let's not waste time here," Greg Hawker said very loudly to Brian, and taking one further shot at the kite he continued on his way.

"Just you wait," Greg shouted from a safe distance. "One day I'll smash it to bits for you!"

Chapter Four

THOSE HEADS AGAIN!

James's father was looking extremely pleased with himself when Jessica and James got back to the old cottage.

"We'll not be short of light tonight," he told them. "I found two gas lanterns under the stairs. I've been down to the local garage and bought a couple of gas cartridges. I can hardly wait until dark to try them out!"

"I thought you bought a really bright light bulb in Wells, Uncle Clive," Jessica said. "Why aren't you using that?"

Mr. Cooper shook his head. "It's a strange fitting I've never seen before," he explained. "It's more like a nightlight than a room light. I should have taken the bulb from the ceiling to make sure. Oh well, this cottage is full of surprises, and I'm starting to think it's rather fun here. Anyway, I guess we're lucky to have electricity here at all!"

James was glad to see his father in such a good mood. Probably his mother was settling in as well. He'd been feeling a bit sorry for his parents. They'd come to Sheppingford obviously expecting to have a good holiday themselves. Certainly he and Jessica were having a good time. The cottage *was* fun, but clearly not what his mother had been expecting. Anyway, now that his father was making the most of it, his mother was hopefully being caught up with his enthusiasm.

James's thoughts suddenly leapt ahead to another subject. "Dad," he said eagerly, "do you think the church will still be open?"

His father frowned and put the unlit lanterns down. "Aren't you going to stay and see how well they work? No, perhaps you're not. The church? You'll have to hurry. It's sure to be locked up soon."

"What's up with you?" Jessica asked. "It's not Sunday, you know!"

"It doesn't have to be Sunday to go into a church," James replied in a very superior way. Then he smiled at Jessica's hurt expression. "I wouldn't mind another look at that old wall painting," he explained. "If it really *does* show Saint Cerig by his well, then the well in the *middle* of the field can't be the real one. There's a sort of wall in the old painting, I'm sure of it. There's no wall in the middle of that field. Surely something would be left there for us to see. I think the well where we found the dog must be the *real* one. The bottom of a rock face like that would be a good place for a building ... wouldn't it?" His voice faded away, because he didn't really know at all. It was just that his idea seemed more likely. There was no notice board up at any of the wells to say which was the right one.

"We'll need my flashlight," Jessica said. "It's nearly dark outside, and we won't know where the light switches are."

The church seemed strangely quiet. The large iron handle on the ancient oak door turned with a sharp *crack*! James crept in first. Jessica came and stood with him. The church felt friendly, but so different from Sunday evening when it had been full and brightly lit.

Gradually they became aware of sounds all around them. Something was clicking in the roof. Various things were creaking, and there was a muffled thud from the direction of the tower. Jessica shone her flashlight on the painting.

The latch cracked, the door creaked. Jessica switched off her flashlight as James turned quickly to see who was coming in. A dark figure stood in the doorway. Without further thought James and Jessica slipped behind the cover of a pillar. The figure paused, then slid noiselessly across the flagstones of the church floor.

It made its way past the James and Jessica and suddenly disappeared. James's heart seemed to stop, and then come back to life with great pounding beats. His eyes searched the gloom but — no one. He could only see Jessica standing next to him.

They waited for some time. Still no noise. James tugged at Jessica's jumper and they left their hiding place. It was very difficult to creep across the uneven stone floor without making even the slightest noise, even in trainers.

They nearly walked into a pillar. This was just where the figure had disappeared. Obviously the "disappearing" figure had walked behind it. So where was it now?

Just as James was wishing he'd stayed in the cottage, the figure turned on a bright flashlight. A hand moved from one part of the old stone pulpit to the next, touching the carved stone heads — the heads that had interested James.

Spellbound, they crept closer until they were only a few feet away. James was sure he could hear the figure breathing. The church door slammed shut.

The figure turned and let out a gasp. Jessica grabbed hold of James's arm in fright. For a moment they stood and stared. Then the flashlight shone brightly into James's eyes and the figure spoke.

"I thought I told you two to keep away! If I thought you were spying on me——"

Jessica stood firm. "Well, we weren't. We just came in here to have a look at the painting. So there! I'd like to know what *you're* up to."

James now felt quite brave himself. What was

Greg Hawker doing in a church he didn't want to come to anyway? "Yes, what *are* you up to?"

Greg Hawker stumbled on his way out of the church in a hurry, not saying anything, leaving James and Jessica none the wiser.

<><><>

After an early breakfast, the Two Jays were out on Fern Hill again. James was holding the kite above his head, and every time the wind tugged at it and pulled his arms out straight, he imagined he was flying high above the Mendips. He'd seen people on paragliders, and promised himself a flight on one when he was old enough. The wind whistled past his ears, blowing his hair this way and that.

"Jessica," he called. "This is a paraglider. I'm going to fly right over the Mendips. I'll see the ground getting smaller until you're just a tiny speck!" He'd flown in planes going on holiday a couple of times, but to be in control would be fantastic. "Well, in my dreams, anyway."

He told Jessica how he could never forget the thrill the first time he'd looked down from the plane and seen the ground like a map. Flying a paraglider was some time in the future, he explained, but flying beneath a massive kite just might be possible – if he only knew how to build one large enough to take his weight!

Jessica's thoughts were more down to earth. Or maybe, she realised, more up to heaven. Before setting out, she'd been reading from her Bible. There was a booklet she used, that set out just a few verses for each day, and helped explain what she read. This morning it had been Isaiah chapter forty. She smiled as she thought of what James had just told her about flying. They both had plenty of energy, but it was good to remember that God wanted to lift her up when things got bad. She could recall the whole verse – for once!

They who wait for the LORD
shall renew their strength;
They shall mount up
with wings like eagles;
They shall run and not be weary;
They shall walk and not faint.

There was a time when she always expected to find something helpful for what she was just about to do – almost like sticking a pin in a page, and finding exactly the verse she needed. She knew she sometimes got real help just when she needed it, but more often help came from remembering something she'd read days, or even weeks earlier. The main thing, she told herself, was to read a bit of her Bible every day, and stay in touch with God.

She was glad to know James felt the same way. He'd told her what had happened eight weeks ago, and quite often they talked about their new life in

God's family. She knew that when you know someone you want to be close to them, and both she and James knew Jesus.

She joined James who was running up the hill. "Stop," she pleaded, for she felt very out of breath now. "I'm going to take a picture of you and the kite with my phone. Stay there, and hold the kite above your head. And it's okay to smile if you want to."

"Thanks," he said, breaking into a grin. "I think I'll take one of you with *my* phone. Okay?"

James knew Jessica was sometimes rude about his results. Even though the picture was there on the screen, somehow the horizon or buildings were often crooked, or feet were mysteriously missing from the bottom of the picture. If she'd been his sister she could hardly have been any ruder! Perhaps, he thought, perhaps it was good thing. It made him really careful before taking a picture. But, then, he reflected, that didn't always seem to do much good!

Jessica took her turn holding the kite for the photograph. James told her to pretend she was having a job to hold it down. A sudden gust of wind made Jessica react quickly, and as she fought with the kite, "click", James was convinced he had a prizewinning photograph on his phone. If it was as fantastic as he expected it to be, he'd enter it in the school handicrafts exhibition in the autumn.

"Come here and look at the screen," he called.

"I've just taken the best one ever!"

"Oh yes?" Jessica asked. "What of? Your thumb?"

James knew she was joking and just snarled at her. "No," he said, "the end of my nose. I had the phone the wrong way round!"

Jessica laughed. "That wouldn't surprise me!"

James was excited about the photograph he'd taken. "I want to get it printed," he said. If he could find a photo shop while on holiday, the result would be sure to leave Jessica speechless.

The wind seemed stronger now. The kite flew well, but there was too much pull on the twin lines. The wind whistled through them, setting up a humming sound. Suddenly the strong pull was gone, and the broken lines drifted in a gentle curve down to the ground. The kite with a short length of line still attached, tossed and turned in the wind until it landed far away in the branches of a large oak tree.

Then the rain came.

Jessica and James turned and fled for the safety of the cottage. At first it looked as though it was only going to be a short, sharp shower, but the pale yellow light on the horizon grew fainter as heavy grey clouds closed in all round them. And then the electricity went off.

With no microwave to help prepare any hot food, Mrs. Cooper had to make a cold lunch by the light from one of the gas lanterns. Jessica said it seemed very cosy eating tuna and salad sandwiches, and cake, by lamplight with the rain beating down outside.

After lunch, Jessica and James were glad of their books. Jessica was reading the one she'd bought in Wells, and James reading one he'd downloaded on his phone.

By the middle of the afternoon the electricity supply was restored, and the horizon started to look brighter again. James pulled his chair over to the window. Every few lines in his book he looked up, hoping to report that the rain had stopped.

By teatime they were resigned to staying in for the rest of the day. Somehow the brightness on the horizon never seemed to get any closer. Then suddenly the heavy grey cloud overhead started to break up, and James and Jessica hurried out to rescue their kite from the oak tree.

That tree was across several fields. The best way would be up the track that led between the quarry and the field with the well. The quarryman – Mr. Slade – was just leaving the quarry. Today he seemed quite pleasant.

He nodded to Jessica and James as though to say "Good evening," and then said, "I don't know what you're both up to, but just make sure you keep away from my stones – and keep away from the water. I wouldn't want you coming to harm." With that he was gone, riding his heavy old bike down the hill towards the village.

"What do you think he meant, James?" Jessica asked. "Was he warning us that there's poison in the water, or was he making some sort of threat?"

James shrugged. "I'm not going to take any notice. I can't see he could hurt us. In any case, we're not going near his miserable old quarry, and we're not going to drink any water from the well. Come on, let's try and get that kite!"

It took nearly an hour to get the kite down from the large oak tree. James had a difficult job getting up to the first branch. He and Jessica found some broken branches and made a sort of ladder. The view from high up was superb. Almost as good as flying. James freed the kite. Twice it caught on the ends of the branches as it fell, but the wind soon blew it free.

Then James had an idea. He had his phone with him. The sun was shining low from beneath the long bank of grey cloud. The grass and hedges sparkled in the warm glow of the evening sun. He would never get up this tree again.

"Remember what I said about taking photographs from kites?" he called down, holding on carefully. "This tree's so high it's just like being up in an aeroplane, or a kite, or a paraglider. Or even a balloon. I'm going to take the most amazing photograph ever."

Once again he took great care to frame the view carefully on the screen. The sun shone sideways across the fields, and the shadows were long and clear. Even the distant Tor at Glastonbury was clear-cut against the retreating clouds. James examined every corner of the screen. The hill, the two wells, Glastonbury Tor. Yes, they were all there.

"Hurry up," Jessica called impatiently from far below.

"Coming down now."

It was good in Sheppingford. Now it was time to go back to the cottage. Tomorrow they were all going to Cheddar. James knew there were caves there. Proper caves. And cheese! But that was tomorrow.

There was so much to be thankful for, and God – God who had made it all and given it to them to enjoy – was the one who should be thanked. James did just that before going to sleep.

Chapter Five

DOWN THE CAVES

"Can we have toast for breakfast today?" James asked the next morning. It was Wednesday. It had rained heavily again in the night.

Jessica followed closely behind her cousin, and sat down at the round kitchen table where James's mother was tipping cornflakes from a large packet. "Oh, yes please, Aunty Amy. I'm ever so fond of toast. I like it warm and soft. Full of lovely country butter."

James made a face. "Horrible," he declared. "I like it all cold and crispy."

Jessica shook her head. "You're meant to butter it while it's still hot. If it's gone crispy then it's been made too long."

James's father reached across and helped himself to the milk. "While you're both arguing I'm going to get on with my breakfast."

Mrs. Cooper laughed. "If you two are going to wait for toast, you're going to be here a long time. How are we going to make toast without a proper cooker?"

"With a toaster?" James suggested, taking the

milk jug from his father.

"No toaster," Jessica pointed out. Then she realised she was being left behind. "Hurry up with the milk," she chided her cousin. "I don't want to be still eating my breakfast when it's time to go."

That made James hurry up. The whole family hurried up. They were planning to get to Cheddar early, to beat the holiday crowds that were sure to be there.

The morning was bright and clear. Far away, the hills that made up the horizon stood out clearly from the blue sky. Everything promised a lovely day.

Jessica thought that the chances of the Cooper family ever making an early start were just about zero. There always seemed to be so much to do at the last moment, in spite of their good intentions. But today they exceeded her expectations by actually leaving on time.

James sat in the back of the car with Jessica and waited for the first sign of Cheddar Gorge. He'd heard so much about the Gorge that it seemed to make it longer in coming. He turned to Jessica but she was looking out of the window. James looked too. Yes, there it was, a large gap cut deeply into the green hills. A massive gap of grey rock and green trees that twisted this way and that as it wound its way to the top of the Mendips.

The Gorge disappeared as the car drew near the

village of Cheddar. Small houses and shops lined the road. They spotted the sign for a car park and found a place in the shade of some trees.

Mr. Cooper went in front and the family followed behind on the narrow pavement. Cars passed them packed with visitors. Jessica watched with dismay. The place would surely be full. They should have made an effort to leave earlier still, but with the Cooper family she realised that was always going to be impossible.

The first car park they walked past was jammed with cars, and so was the next one, so she could see they'd done well to park in the first place they found. People pushed past her as though she wasn't going fast enough. Jessica wanted to hurry along, but James's father led the way at a steady pace. Then all of a sudden they were in the bottom part of Cheddar Gorge.

Crowds of people in summer dresses and beachwear gazed through plate-glass windows at rows of souvenirs in the gift shops. Jessica looked too. She wanted to take something nice back for her parents. They'd given her some holiday money and she wasn't going to spend it all on herself.

A glass vase caught her eye. She turned to ask James's mother what she thought of it. Then she realised she was on her own. In a moment of panic she could see nothing but crowds of pushing holidaymakers, all trying to get a closer look at the window. James and his parents must have gone on up the road. She could try phoning James. But no, surely they couldn't have gone far enough to be out of sight.

"Are you coming in?" James was leaning out of the shop doorway.

Jessica could have mangled him. "Just a minute," she called, having no intention of letting him guess what she'd been thinking.

"I'm going to buy a skeleton," James told her. He pointed to a long, white, realistic model dangling at the top of the window.

"Trust you!" Jessica said. "I'm going to buy something nice to take home for Mum and Dad."

"When it's dark tonight," James continued, taking no notice of his cousin, "I'm going to come into your room and let its legs brush against your face. When you wake up I'll shine a torch on it and you'll scream and scream and scream."

Mrs. Cooper came up to them, smiling. "That's right. You discuss what you're going to get. Something nice is it, James?"

"It's nasty," Jessica said. "Horrid and nasty, just like James."

James's mother looked at the window and then back at James — quickly. "It's not a skeleton, is it? I'm not having one of those in the cottage!"

"Oh, Mum," James said with a groan. "It's not a *real* one. Jessica wants to have one too, so she can take it to bed with her every night."

Jessica let out a gasp. "James! How could you?"

"I'm sorry," James replied innocently. "Did I misunderstand you?"

Jessica turned to James's mother and decided to ignore her rude cousin. "Aunty Amy, do you think my mum and dad would like that glass vase? See? That green and brown one at the back?"

Mrs. Cooper looked at the vase and then at Jessica. "Well...." She sounded very uncertain. "I don't think it's quite what.... How about something a bit more local? A piece of local pottery."

Jessica nodded. "I know what you mean. There's a frog there. It says, 'A present from Cheddar', on its back." She screwed up her nose. "I don't think my mum likes frogs."

"Get it for yourself," James suggested. "Put it in your bed, and when you get in, it will feel ever so cold and real."

"James!" his mother said. "I'll not have you teasing Jessica like that. How would *you* like a frog in *your* bed?"

"It would be all right," James said, "as long as it didn't keep croaking all night."

"We'll see," Jessica said, feeling like fighting back now. "I know where one lives. Just behind the large stone inside the cottage gate. You'd better look carefully before you get into bed tonight!"

James felt silenced. He reached in his pocket

and took out enough money to pay for the skeleton. When it was safely in its bag, he went out into the bright sunlight to wait for Jessica to make up her mind.

Jessica was unable to make up her mind. An ornament would be more for her mother than for her father. Besides, they'd never been to Cheddar as far as she knew, so they wouldn't want a souvenir. A souvenir was something to help you remember a place, and you couldn't remember a place if you'd never been there. No, that couldn't be right ... or could it? Jessica left the shop in despair. There would be plenty more shops as they walked up the Gorge.

James saw a shop that sold digital cameras and offered a printing service.

DIGITAL PRINTS WITHIN THE HOUR
LARGE PRINTS TWENTY-FOUR
HOUR SERVICE

James felt in the pocket of his jeans for his phone.

"Are we coming back here at all?" he asked his father. "I've got two amazing holiday pictures on my phone, and I want a really large print from each. Twenty-four hours? We don't want to wait around in Cheddar that long!"

"We?" his father asked. "They're your

photographs, remember. You could always get the bus back here tomorrow!"

James knew his father was only teasing him and he laughed. "I'm sure it's worth coming back here to Cheddar again. I'll be able to pay for them with some of my holiday money. How's that?"

"Come on," his father said, pushing him gently through the doorway. "I'm sure we'll be back, and I'll pay. You know I've got a heart of gold. I've also bought tickets for one of the caves online."

"Brilliant, Dad," James said, to the amusement of others in the small shop.

The woman at the counter let James transfer the two pictures he wanted using Bluetooth, and took out a pad to make a note of James's name. "Lunch-time tomorrow," she said, "but you have to pay in advance."

"Why's that?" James asked in surprise.

"It's because this is a holiday place," the woman explained pleasantly. "We get quite a few people who never bother to call back. So we say 'payment in advance' and then it doesn't matter if we never see them again."

"I just hope your father isn't wasting his money with those two masterpieces," Jessica said, hiding a smile.

James pretended not to hear. He smiled at the woman and turned to leave the shop. "Can we go down the caves now? You never know, Jessica might manage to get lost!"

A bit further up the road a queue was forming outside the entrance to the show cave Mr. Cooper had booked for. A man on the pavement was telling people that in five minutes' time they'd be taken down it. James and Jessica ran on to reserve a place in the fast-growing crowd.

James's father reached them first and held up a finger in caution. "Make sure you keep close to us. We don't want you falling down any holes."

Several people turned and smiled, and James started to feel awkward. As if he'd do a thing like that!

A group of people emerged from the cave and everyone stood to one side to let them pass. James tried to peer into the blackness but there was nothing to see. Cold, damp air came out with the people who were leaving. It was all very exciting.

"This way, please," the guide called. "I want you all to stay close to me, and please no wandering off on your own. Now then, ladies and gentlemen, you are entering...."

But James wasn't listening. The sound of running water, the lights twinkling out from the darkest places imaginable, the coldness of the air and the smell of damp earth and rock – he was in world of his own. He was a caveman, exploring dangerous territory for the first time. Could there be cave bears and hyenas waiting round the next turn of the narrow cave? Would men from another tribe be waiting to club him to death? Dare he go on and find out?

"If you could all stand over here by the electric light," the guide continued, "I'll show you some interesting shapes on the walls."

"Electric light?" James said aloud. All his imaginings were taken away by the very mention of electricity. Gone were the burning rushes providing his light, while frightening away the wild animals. Several people pushed and shoved in the dim light, and James found himself at the back.

Suddenly the guide turned the lights out and James was glad he wasn't alone. One by one the lights came on again as the guide pointed out strange shapes high on the cave walls. It was interesting, but James decided he'd be quite glad to be back outside in the warmth and daylight, even though the guide managed to make everything sound exciting.

The guide explained that there were many more passages than the general public were allowed to explore. Deep down under the Gorge there were passages that filled with water at times of heavy rain. Cavers had used special dye to trace where these underground rivers came from, and where they went.

As quickly as it had started, the trip was over, and there at the entrance was another crowd waiting for their turn to visit the wonderland of nature deep in the cliffs of Cheddar Gorge.

The air felt so warm that James found himself gasping for breath. He was glad they'd been down, but also glad to be back in the safety of the Gorge. A car sounded its horn loudly as he stepped backwards into the road. Safe? Cavemen never had to put up with dangers like this!

Chapter Six

THE NEXT DISCOVERY

James dug his knife deep into the marmalade jar the next morning. "I like having breakfast on holiday," he announced as he scooped the marmalade onto the bread. "You can use your knife in the jars instead of a spoon. That's the sort of thing that makes a holiday so good."

His mother looked into the jar and saw the thick line of butter left from the knife. "I don't know where you got that idea, my lad. You've got some disgusting habits." She smiled. "That reminds me. It's high time you had a long bath, instead of a shower."

Jessica was going to laugh out loud but she stopped herself in time. James's mother sounded serious about it. What could she mean? They surely weren't expected to bath in Saint Cerig's well, or any of the other so-called wells! They were the only places she could think of, apart from the pond in Farmer Osborne's farmyard. It wouldn't be that. You'd come out of there dirtier and smellier than you were before you went in!

"What sort of bath?" was all Jessica could say.

Her Aunty Amy continued smiling. "Haven't you seen the bath?"

"There isn't one," James insisted. He thought for a moment, and frowned. "There's only a shower room built onto the back, and the outside toilet."

"You go out into the yard and you'll see it," his mother said. "It's a big tin bath and it hangs on the wall."

James looked horrified. "I thought that was keeping logs in. We couldn't bath out there! It would be too cold with water from the outside tap. We'd all freeze to death!"

His mother was laughing now. "What a pair you both are. When Granny was very young, it was all *she* to bath in. Once a week her father would fetch the bath in from the coal house, and put it in front of the fire. She once told me she never thought anything of it at the time, but I suppose it does seem rather strange now. She says she wasn't very old when the family went all posh and had a bathroom built onto the back of the house."

James had never heard of this before. "You mean the house where Granny lives now? I thought it *always* had a bathroom."

His mother shook her head. "It was built on long before I was born. Listen carefully. What you've got to do is fill the bucket and kettle with water and put them on the gas hob after lunch. By the evening the water should be warm enough.

We'll all go for a walk and leave you to have your bath tonight. I'm quite sure you'll need one the most."

"Cheek!" James muttered. "All right, if I'm going to risk pneumonia in the yard, I'm going to get really dirty today. I'm going to go digging in the ground round what we think is Saint Cerig's well. There's stacks of rubbish to clear away."

"You don't bath in the yard," his mother explained, smiling. "We'll bring the bath indoors before we fill it, and you can go on scrubbing until you're clean, or until the water goes cold. It will be Jessica's turn tomorrow – if she needs one. Being a girl she might be cleaner."

"She won't be," James said. "If we're going to clear all the rubbish round the well, she'll need one tonight. In fact," he added generously, "she can have my turn, and I'll use the shower."

His father was trying not to laugh.

"What's so funny?" James asked.

"It's a joke," his father said, laughing out loud. "You should have seen your face when Mum told you to fill the bucket and kettle with water! No, you stick with the shower." He shook his head, still laughing. "If we'd come to this cottage a few years ago, that tin bath probably *was* the only way to keep clean. Now, are you sure you want to explore around that old well today? I'd thought of going back to Cheddar and exploring further up the

Gorge. How about it?"

James groaned. "Tomorrow?" he asked. "Can we go tomorrow instead?"

Mr. Cooper finished his mug of coffee and frowned. He turned to his wife. "I suppose we could go on our own. James and Jessica should be all right just for the afternoon. We could mention it to the minister, and if these two need anything they could always go there. What do you think?"

Before his mother could answer, James let out a loud, "Yes *please*. Do say 'yes', Mum. *Please!*"

His mother nodded. "No mischief, mind. No going anywhere dangerous."

"There isn't anywhere dangerous," James assured her. "Only the old mineshaft, and we won't try and go down there." As soon as he'd said it, he wished he'd kept quiet. They wouldn't have tried to go down it anyway, but now his mother looked worried.

His father smoothed things over, and the arrangements were made. James's parents would be around until late morning, and be back by early evening. All James and Jessica had to do was to keep away from the old mineshaft. There would be food ready for them in the fridge, to eat whenever they felt hungry.

They ran quickly up the small lane, their first destination being the old quarry where Mr. Slade seemed to have some sort of secret. Why else did he want them to keep away?

They were soon there, but approached cautiously. No, there was no sign of Mr. Slade. The whole place looked deserted.

"There's not much here really," James observed in disgust. "No machinery or anything like in a proper quarry."

"But it's not a proper quarry," his cousin said. "Only Mr. Thing works it. He wouldn't need diggers and stuff. He probably just chips the rocks out by hand."

James looked at a pile of freshly broken stone on the uneven floor of the quarry. "I can't think what he makes from this sort of stone. It doesn't even——"

"Here's the mineshaft," Jessica called out loudly from where she was now doing some exploration.

"Then keep away," James warned. "You know what we promised my parents."

Jessica laughed. "All right, but there's not much danger. You couldn't fall down very far, even if you wanted to."

James joined her, and from a safe distance they stood and looked. There was a large hole filled almost to the top with old bricks, plaster and general builders' rubble. A small stream, probably caused by the heavy rain yesterday, trickled its way through the top layer and disappeared.

James shook his head. "That's that, then.

Nobody's been using it as a mine. Not for years and years."

Jessica looked excited. "Supposing the water down there is poisoned. It might drain out of here into the wells and springs in the fields below here."

"Brilliant, Jessica. You're right, the poison *could* be coming from here. But there's no way we can check it out."

Jessica said she thought there must surely be a way. "But I don't know how," she added.

James looked around to see if there were any clues. "What's under that tarpaulin?"

The green sheet was covering something large and lumpy. It was held down along the edges with several rocks. "Let's see."

Jessica hesitated. "Do you think we ought to?"

"Just a peep and then we'll go. We can lift up the corner here. It's nearly loose anyway." James pulled it back.

The tarpaulin had been put over some large stones, most of which had been cut into various shapes.

"That must be what Mr. Slade does here," James decided out loud "They're probably for a wall or fireplace or something. Come on, let's get over to our well."

Jessica had to agree with him. "There's nothing more we can do here. Yes, let's go and see if we can dig up old Saint Cerig."

James screwed up his nose. “No thanks! Just his well – and his chapel if we can find it.”

They took the track out of the quarry, and went to cross the lane to go down into the field with the well amongst the trees. James said he was convinced that was the proper site for Saint Cerig’s well. The other site in the open field surely wasn’t the sort of place anyone would build a chapel. It was a shame nobody knew for sure.

Mr. Peterson, the minister, was passing in his car and he stopped for a chat in the lane. James explained his idea about the well by the rock face being the original. Mr. Peterson looked interested.

“I’ve sometimes wondered that myself. I’ve only been here in Sheppingford five years, so I don’t know how it would go down with the older people if I spoilt one of their traditions! I can see you like mysteries, so we can share it as a secret – unless you can come up with definite proof.”

“We like *solving* mysteries,” James agreed. “Who doesn’t!”

Mr. Peterson seemed pleased. “Then here’s another one for you both. When you were in the church on Sunday, did you notice the two small stone heads let into the old pulpit? I’m sure you must have done.”

“Bill and Ben!” James coughed and felt himself going red. He laughed. “That’s what I called them to myself. I, er....”

Mr. Peterson laughed with him. "I must remember that. Well, there was something in the local paper last week about Bill and Ben ... about the *stone heads,"* he corrected himself, and laughed. "There was a photograph too. The heads are supposed to have come from another local church but no one knows which one. Tradition has it that they'd have a tale to tell if they could talk! You'd be surprised how many visitors we've had this week. A lot of holiday folk must have read the local paper. Anyway, the heads haven't talked yet, so no one is any the wiser!"

James could understand now why Greg had taken it into his mind to go to the church on Monday night. After all he'd been saying against the church he could hardly go there while it was still light. But what *would* the heads say if they could talk?

James knew that old traditions were always interesting, and there was often quite a bit of truth in them in a tangled sort of way. Mr. Peterson had told them that nearly seven hundred years ago Saint Cerig had once built a chapel or something by his well. The old wall painting in the church certainly showed a stone wall, although the painting had been done a hundred or so years later.

"I saw your father a few minutes ago, James" the minister said. "I know they're going back to Cheddar, so if you need anything when your parents are out, don't mind asking. My wife and I will be in the whole time. I have some writing to do."

The Two Jays thanked him and were soon alone. First they made their way down to the "official" well in the middle of the field. Some flat stones had been laid around a spring of clear water. Long green weeds waved in the gentle current that now swirled around the small pool. Within a few yards the water sank back through the soggy turf.

"Come on," Jessica said impatiently, "let's go and see *our* well – the proper one."

Their well near the rock face looked much more interesting. The recent rain had turned it from a stagnant pool to an active one. James thought that calling things like this a well was a strange thing to do. He'd always thought of wells as deep holes in the ground, like the old mineshaft, where you had to use a bucket on a rope to get the water up. The wells round here were more like springs, with the rock hollowed out so the water collected in a deep pool before running away.

The rock face was pale grey and the water looked extremely cold and inviting on such a warm day. Was the water still poisoned? James felt himself draw away at the thought. Could it have poisoned Farmer Osborne's sheepdog and his sheep? The water looked so pure and....

"Brushwood killer!" he said suddenly.

Jessica jumped back in alarm. *"Where?"*

"That's what the man from the Environment Agency thought had poisoned the animals. What's missing here?" James asked.

"Nothing. There's plenty of water. Why, what's wrong?"

"No plants in the water," James said. "Remember how they were moving around in the other well?" He bent down and looked closely into the water. "There are some dead plants in the bottom. This water's poisoned with brushwood killer. What more proof do we need?"

Jessica had been thinking. "It doesn't mean.... Yes, it does. Well, it means it was once poisoned by *something*! But maybe it's not poisoned *now*."

"We'll let Farmer Osborne know what we've found. This well ought to be fenced off."

As he stepped back, James nearly trod on a rabbit, its eyes open and staring, its legs stretched out straight. Flies were buzzing round its head. No! It was too awful to think about. It was a hot day, and he and Jessica could have tried drinking some of that water if they hadn't been warned.

James scuffed some leaves over the rabbit and said nothing to Jessica. She'd be really upset if she knew. He wouldn't pick it up in case it had died from some infectious disease. Or could it be poisoned? That would make some sort of sense. Some farmer — not Farmer Osborne surely? — had been careless with their chemicals.

James started thinking out loud. “Perhaps large quantities of Framer Osborne’s brushwood killer got into the water supply all round here.”

“I’d been thinking the same,” Jessica said. “But if it had, all the grass near the little springs and the marshy areas would be dead. But it’s not. It’s a real mystery.”

James was lost in thought. Hadn’t the inspector from the Environment Agency thought of that? Yes, of course, the Agency had more or less decided it *was* Farmer Osborne’s brushwood killer, even though they could find no trace of it in the water when they carried out their tests. And yet.... James frowned and watched the water moving gently in the well.

All right, so the poison *might* have been Farmer Osborne’s fault. There was nothing more they could do. He had no intention of tasting the water to find out if it was still poisoned!

“I still think that mineshaft is somehow to blame,” Jessica said. “But, as you said, there’s no way we can check it.”

James examined the rock face carefully. It seemed so smooth. It didn’t look as though someone had chipped it flat. More likely it had been polished by a moving glacier in the Ice Age, when the caves were formed. There could almost be a pattern in the rock. He pulled some of the ivy away and ... yes, it certainly looked like some sort of carved pattern. There were two deeply cut holes, one on each side.

"Come and see, Jessica. I'm sure there's something carved on this rock face!"

Jessica helped him to pull away more of the ivy. Showers of dirt fell into their hair. Jessica laughed and put her head down to the ground and shook it hard. "Perhaps we'll need that old tin bath tonight after all," she joked.

Soon they stood back to have a good look. "Who'd want to carve a picture on a rock like this?" Jessica asked.

"It might have been part of Saint Cerig's chapel," James suggested. He felt excited.

Jessica frowned. "This rock is part of the hill. It hasn't been built here by anyone."

"Perhaps the chapel was built up against it."

"Perhaps. But where are the walls?"

James stepped closer again. "It might not have been a *stone* chapel. It might have been built with branches and goat skins or something."

"Goat skins?" Jessica started kicking into the leaves that covered the ground. "I can feel some lumps. Here, get me something to dig into these leaves."

James set to work with a small piece of flat stone, scraping away the soft earth. There was a line of stones under the leaves. Foundations?

"Look, over there!" Jessica shouted excitedly.

James looked to where his cousin was pointing. A pile of earth and stones was half hidden by a large holly bush.

James was there first. He pulled out three large stones. "They're cut smooth for building," he observed. "Look here, there are there round holes in the middle of some of them. See? That's weird. I suppose they *could* be part of an old chapel, but there aren't very many."

"Let's pull a few more out," Jessica suggested, already getting her hands round one of them.

They set to work willingly, turning over stones covered in wet earth and dead leaves.

Jessica saw something shining among the earth and stones. It was the neck of an old glass bottle. She'd seen one like it in an antique shop. The glass was slightly green and uneven. The part where the stopper belonged was nothing like any modern bottle. It was much fatter and had a glass marble wedged in the top. She showed it to James, who immediately pulled out some small pieces of china.

"It looks like we've found an old rubbish dump," he said.

"Pass me that stick," Jessica said, and she began poking around in the soft earth.

There was a broken lid from a toothpaste jar. The writing on the pottery lid said *Cherry Tooth Paste*, and there was part of a picture of a woman's face showing on their piece. There was no sign of the rest of it.

James found some broken stems from clay pipes, and then they seemed to have unearthed everything. They were obviously not going to find any valuable treasure.

"Come on," he said, the impatient one for once. "Let's get on with the work we came to do."

Jessica had to agree. "Anyway," she said, putting their finds carefully to one side, "there might be some more right at the bottom."

James nodded. "Clear this lot yourself, and anything you find can be your reward!"

Jessica stood up and looked at the six large stones they'd managed to unearth. "Do you think they could be from a building that was here once upon a time? A chapel?"

James surveyed the few stones. "Seven hundred years ago it might have been. It looks a sorry sight now."

Jessica stood with him. "We could sort all the stones out and see if there are enough," she suggested.

"Enough for what? There aren't nearly enough to build anything."

Jessica looked excited but rather puzzled. "It might have been very small," she said.

James shook his head. "Do you really think we should try and sort them out?"

"We could try. Tell you what, it's time for lunch now. We'll come back this afternoon when your parents are at Cheddar. We'll bring some scrubbing brushes and an old tin for water. There's a spade in the shed in the back yard. The first thing to do will be to clean these stones. We can't lift some of the big ones, but we can push them about if we're careful."

Chapter Seven

THE ACCIDENT

There was a note on the table when they got back to the cottage. James's parents had decided to leave early, but they would be back in plenty of time for tea. Their lunch of fresh bread, Cheddar cheese and tomatoes had been left ready as arranged, but James and Jessica were too excited to want to eat much. However, they ate the lot, because James said they would need all the energy they could find!

In the note, James's father promised to call and collect the two large prints from James's phone. That was yet another bit of excitement for James.

As they left the cottage door, they could see someone running down the hill towards the cottage. Running wildly and shouting.

The figure got closer. Yes, of course. James recognised him immediately. It was Greg Hawker, the older one of the Ghastly Two. He seemed excited or upset about something.

Greg rushed through the cottage gate. "You've got to come quick!" he shouted in his strong Somerset voice. "It's Brian!"

"Where?" James asked.

Greg sounded really frightened. "Just up the hill. Be quick!"

"What's happened?" Jessica asked.

"It were an accident. I swear it."

"Is he badly hurt?" Jessica was turning pale.

"Hurt, or dead maybe. It *were* an accident." Greg started to look dazed.

James didn't feel too good himself. It had all happened so suddenly.

"It's his neck," Gregg said quietly, his face white. "He fell out of the tree."

"Is he breathing?" Jessica asked in alarm, picturing Brian with a broken neck.

Greg nodded.

James realised that something had to be done — quickly. If Brian was lying out on the hill he would need to be kept warm, and one of them would have to phone for an ambulance.

"Jessica," he said, "run upstairs and get the blankets off my bed."

"You'd better be quick," Gregg urged. "He be bleeding ever such a lot."

"I'll get the blankets," Jessica said, "but I don't think I like the thought of blood. Can I stay and wait here for the ambulance?" She was already dialling 999 on her phone. "You can go back with Greg, James. Okay?" She desperately wanted to help, but knew perfectly well she would be no help out on the hill.

The emergency operator on the phone wanted details of exactly where the accident had taken place, and Jessica passed her phone to Greg. "You tell them," she said. "I'm going to get the blankets."

While Greg spoke to the operator, Jessica emerged from upstairs with the blankets from James's bed. James had decided exactly what they should do. "Jessica, run as fast as you can to the minister's house. Tell him what's happened, and when the ambulance arrives you can explain where they have to go."

"Should I phone your mum and dad and get them to come back?" Jessica asked.

James shook his head. "There's no point in worrying them. The ambulance will be here and gone long before they can get back"

"I think there's a box of first aid things on the kitchen shelf," Jessica called as she hurried out through the gate on her way to the vicarage.

James didn't stay to watch her go. He grabbed the box from the shelf, and with Greg leading the way they ran onto the hill, taking deep breaths as they went.

As the hill got steeper, they had to slow down. Greg kept saying, "It were an accident, see. It *were* an accident."

Brian was lying under a large oak tree. Greg must have put his jacket over him, but it had fallen off with all the twisting about.

"It's all right, young 'un," Greg told him. "I've got some help. You'll soon be all right."

James looked at Brian Tucker's throat. From the way he was moving his head around, at least his neck didn't seem to be broken. The sight of the oozing blood made him heave deeply inside. "Please, Lord, make me able to help," he prayed.

A handkerchief had been loosely tied round Brian's neck. It was stained deep red. There was no point in asking questions. Greg's catapult lay on the ground by Brian's side. James kept reminding himself that he'd come to help. He'd be no help if he just stayed looking. Better not to look. Better just to try to get on with trying to help. James opened the first aid box. Inside he found a small bandage, sticking plaster, antiseptic ointment and some cotton wool.

James turned to Greg. "You'd better do this. I've never done any proper first aid before." He held out one of the bandages.

Greg didn't move. He didn't even shake his head.

"Come on," James pleaded. He pushed the bandage into Greg's hands. "Please!"

Greg just stared at him. James sighed and took the bandage back. "Please help me, Jesus," he whispered aloud. "Please help me to do it properly." When this was over, he was quite sure he would try to learn just a bit about first aid. All he could do now was try to stop the bleeding. An ambulance might be half an hour. Perhaps more.

Cautiously, and feeling sick, James untied the handkerchief. The deep wound was a long gash that didn't seem to have been made with a stone from the catapult. James went to wipe the blood away from Brian's neck, but realised that the blood was already clotting and so helping to stem the flow. He was alarmed to see that Brian was losing interest in what was going on. Perhaps it would be best not to do anything but wrap him up gently in the blankets.

Brian looked up as James tucked the blankets under his side. "Thanks," he croaked.

James sat down by Brian's side. "You lie still and the ambulance will soon be here."

"That's right," Gregg told him. He was now biting his nails nervously. He flicked the hair away from his eyes. "There's not much else we can do."

"We *could* all pray," James said.

Brian opened his eyes for a moment. "Yes, please."

"Can if you want to," Greg muttered.

James stayed where he was by Brian's side. "Lord," he began nervously, "we ask you to keep Brian safe. We——"

"It's a bit late for that," Gregg interrupted.

James felt himself going red. It was difficult to pray out loud like this. "Jesus," he said suddenly, "please let Brian be all right. Please make the ambulance come quickly. Please help Brian to get better quickly. Please, Lord Jesus, please!"

Even Greg was apparently moved by this short prayer, for he said Amen quietly, and Brian said, "Thank you."

"Now, you just lie still," James said. He turned to Greg. "How did it happen?"

Greg shook his head and looked miserable. "You ain't going to believe this."

"I might," James said, but he felt he probably wouldn't.

"It weren't the catapult," Greg said quickly, as he saw where James was looking. "Nothing to do with that thing. Brian were up in this oak tree here. I told him to get on out of it, and he just fell. Fell right here, but he caught his neck on that broken bit of branch." Greg pointed up at the oak tree, but James kept looking down at the catapult and wondering if this was the truth.

Greg put his foot over the catapult and looked guilty. "Up there," he said pointing into the oak tree. "Right against that broken branch he fell. Then on down to the ground."

"Nothing to do with the catapult then?" James asked.

Greg kicked the catapult down the hill. "No, just like I told you. I swear."

James nodded. "Okay."

Greg turned on him, accusingly. "You don't

believe me, do you!"

Brian opened his eyes again and said, "That's right, it *were* an accident."

"One of us had better go back down the hill and keep an eye open for the ambulance," James said. He had no idea what to make of it. "I'll go if you like, Greg. As soon as help arrives, I'll be back."

As he ran back down he heard the emergency siren, and very soon three paramedics were making their way up the hill. James went back up with them.

Brian was lying where James had left him, but there was no sign of Greg.

"Greg's gone," Brian said.

While James explained who Greg Hawker was, one of the paramedics knelt down and examined Brian's neck. He spent some time in bandaging it.

"Where's Greg gone?" he asked at last.

"Dunno," Brian said, staring in fright at the paramedic. "He just runned off."

The paramedic nodded. "He must have been afraid of getting caught."

"It weren't his fault," Brian said quickly. "It were an accident, see. I just fell out of the tree."

"Then why has he run off?" the paramedic asked.

"Perhaps he was frightened," James suggested.

The paramedic stood up and walked over to James. "This is the one who's frightened," he said quietly. "You don't need to be a paramedic to see he's afraid to say what really happened, for fear of what the other boy might do to him. I'm getting the police here. One thing is certain, Greg Hawker has *got* to be found!"

Chapter Eight

NOISES IN THE NIGHT

That evening, disaster struck in the holiday cottage. James's mother was the first to notice damp patches on the landing ceiling. Although it hadn't rained that day, there had been heavy rain the previous night.

"I don't think it will matter," she said, and the whole family went down to have their evening meal, which turned out to be four ready meals from the microwave.

James's father had collected the two large prints from James's phone, and they were even better than James dared hope from looking at the small images on the screen.

James put the prints on the table. The photo of Jessica trying to hold the kite on the hill was just perfect, but the view he'd taken from the oak tree was even——

Crash! Something heavy had fallen upstairs. James was up first but there was nothing to be seen. Jessica's wardrobe was standing against the wall. He'd been quite sure it had fallen over. His parents' and Jessica's beds were still in one piece.

What could it have been? Then he looked into his own miniature bedroom.

"Oh no! Oh, Dad, the ceiling's fallen down! All over my bed!"

James lay on the old sofa downstairs and yawned. When he thought back on it, it did seem rather funny. Lucky, too, that Jessica had taken his blankets to put round Brian. A lot of water had come through with the ceiling plaster. Nothing had been ruined — except the ceiling — and his father had phoned the owner. His parents would have insisted on alternative accommodation, but James and Jessica managed to convince them to say they'd stay put, as long as nothing dramatic happened to the other ceilings.

For the rest of the holiday James would have to sleep downstairs on the sofa, and that was a bit of fun really. It would be something to tell his friends at school. Not many of them would have had a ceiling fall down on their beds during the holidays!

James turned over and tried to get comfortable. The gap between the two seat cushions was in the wrong place, and the cushion edges dug into his hip. He listened. Not a sound from above. Jessica would probably be asleep by now, in her cosy bed. His mind kept turning to the possibility of poisoned water in the well. It was a good thing the tap water was safe to drink.

He thought of the water running through the cave in Cheddar Gorge. The guide had said something about tracing the course of the underground rivers using dye. He hadn't been able to hear properly from the back. If they could find a harmless dye, they might be able to find where the water came from, that fed the wells and streams round about.

They could put it into one of the streams further up the hill and see if it changed the colour of the water at Saint Cerig's well – both his wells! James yawned. It was too hard to plan this sort of thing so late. He yawned again and was soon fast asleep.

That was strange. He was wide awake at once. It must be very late now. He seemed to have been asleep for ages. It sounded like someone knocking. He sat up in bed, his heart beating rapidly with fright. He pressed his phone to light up the time. Nearly twenty to one. No one would be calling here this late.

There it was again. It certainly sounded like someone. He wouldn't wake his parents yet, in case it was something silly like a hedgehog at the door.

The knocking had stopped now. There was only the sound of the wind echoing down the kitchen chimney. That sounded weird enough without having knocking noises as well. He slid back under the blankets. Now there was a different sound. Like something rattling. This needed investigating.

He would creep to the front door, listen, and then creep back. Getting out of his temporary bed, he opened the door quietly, and *there was someone standing in the hall!*

"Who is it?" A silly question, but he knew he had to say something. It was funny how you remembered things in a moment of panic. A school teacher had once told him to say nothing, if he couldn't think of anything sensible to say. That teacher should be here now!

"It's me – Jessica – of course," came a whisper. "I thought I heard someone down here. Was it you?"

James shook his head in the darkness. "No, I've only just.... Listen!" The rattling came again, much louder this time.

"It's the letterbox," Jessica said. "Someone's using it as a knocker."

"Go and see who it is," James suggested. He tried to control a shiver. Strange, he didn't feel cold.

"You go!" Jessica retorted rather indistinctly.

By the faint light coming through the window, James noticed she was chewing the neck of her pyjama top.

"Let's both go," he suggested. "We won't open the door. Just speak through the letterbox."

At the front door they paused. Whoever or whatever it was, was still there.

"Who is it?" Jessica called loudly, making

James jump.

"Let me in," an urgent voice said.

Jessica caught hold of James's arm. "It's Greg Hawker. Shall we let him in?"

"Of course." James had his hand already on the bolt.

Greg came in slowly. Jessica led him into the small living room where James had been sleeping, and turned on the dim ceiling light. Greg looked even more untidy than usual, and his eyes were wide and staring.

"They won't believe me," he said in a hoarse voice. "I know they won't. They kept saying I'd get into trouble with that catapult. I knew different, and now ... see, I've got it coming to me, that's for sure. I daren't go back home. My dad would skin me alive." His voice kept getting louder. "I thought of running away, but they'd only catch me. You saw Bri. Do you think he'll be all right?"

"I should think so," James said. "I'll go and wake my dad up. He'll know what to do. He knows what happened on the hill with Brian."

As James turned to climb the stairs, Greg pulled him back with a powerful grip. "No grownups," he whispered. "I don't want no grownups." He tightened his grip on James's arm. "They're the ones what makes all the trouble."

"Not my dad," James protested. "He'll help you, honest he will."

But Greg was insistent. "No grownups!"

James felt Greg let go of his arm. In spite of all his bluster, Greg Hawker seemed so helpless standing there in the living room. "You'd be best back at your home," James advised.

"I daren't go back." Greg shook his head, scattering his hair in all directions. "Look here, you two have *got* to help me. No one will think of looking for me here. You'd better not tell anybody."

"We can't do that," James said.

Greg pulled himself up straight. He seemed much taller than either of the Two Jays. "Look, I'm telling you straight. You shelter me here, or it will be the worse for you!"

"We can't. Anyway, my mum and dad would find you," James said, backing away a little. He went into the kitchen, and Greg followed. Jessica came with them and closed the door. The three of them sat down at the old kitchen table.

"Surely your father would try and help you," James said. "Besides, don't you want to find out about Brian?"

Greg's tough expression softened a little. "Yes, I suppose I do." He pointed at James. *"You* find out how he is!"

"No, not me," James said. "You!"

Greg moved in his chair as though he was about to stand up. "I'm telling you to do it!" He sat back again and sighed. "What's the use? I'm in for it anyway. If I go to my dad, he'll kill me. Brian's mother would be no better."

"What about Mr. Peterson, the minister?" James suggested.

Greg looked surprised. "What, Holy Dan? You wouldn't catch me near *him*! You're almost as bad. Praying up there on the hill like that!"

"I was praying for Brian," James said. "Remember? You were glad at the time."

"I might have been," Greg admitted. "That sort of thing's more for Brian. When you'd gone he said he'd try and be a good Christian – if God would let him live. It's all rubbish if you ask me!" Greg sounded quite worked up now.

"Well it's not!" James said boldly, surprising even himself. "You think whatever you like. I *know* it's not rubbish."

Greg hesitated a moment before saying, "Don't know anything about that sort of thing. Look here, what are you going to do for me now? I don't want no sermons."

"I still think you could go to – what do you call him? – Holy Dan."

"I can't," Greg insisted, "and I won't."

"Then I'm going up to get my dad," James said, hoping this would make Greg see some sense.

"Perhaps I *will* go and see him." Greg got slowly to his feet. "As long as you both come too, mind."

James turned to Jessica who'd been listening

silently. She was squeezing her toes with her fingers to warm them up. The flag-stone floor in the kitchen was so cold!

"I'll go and throw on some clothes," she whispered, because by now she was sure James's parents would wake up. Greg had raised his voice several times.

"You stay in the cottage, Jessica" James said. "I don't think you'd better be out as late as this."

"No," Greg said sharply. "She comes too, see."

"Then I'm staying here with her," was James's equally sharp reply.

"Don't be so silly," Jessica chided. "As long as we're all together, no harm will come to us. I'll soon be dressed, and we can leave a short note explaining where we've gone."

Greg shook his head. "No notes."

"Only in case James's parents come down and wonder where we are."

"No notes," Greg repeated.

Jessica shook her head firmly. "Then no us. Leaving a note is only being sensible."

"Okay, just a short note," Greg agreed grudgingly. "And you tear it up when you gets back if no one's seen it."

Ten minutes later Mr. Peterson was surprised to see the three of them at his front door. He looked at them sleepily before inviting them in. Along with everyone else in the village, he'd heard about

Brian's accident.

"Who knows you're here?" he asked.

"No one," James said when they were in the hallway of the vicarage. He explained how Greg had made them come alone.

The minister turned to Greg. "You were extremely unwise to run off like that."

"I never done it," Greg said quickly. "It were an accident. I swear it were." He looked back at the front door and scuffed his feet.

"That's what Brian says, and I'm not going to argue with you," Mr. Peterson said.

"You're not?" Greg sounded surprised.

"Not if you say so, and if Brian says the same."

"Then you'll tell my dad that?" Greg asked. He looked more at ease now.

Mr. Peterson sounded more serious than Jessica and James had ever heard him sound. "It's not as easy as that, Greg. It would have been, if you hadn't run off. As it is, Brian's mother is likely to make an official complaint to the police."

Greg looked at the minister in horror. "The police? She's never going to do that?"

"That's why I said you'd been unwise. If you'd stayed to explain to the police what had happened instead of disappearing — well, what was everyone to think?"

"But *you* know," Greg insisted.

"Even if I say I believe you, not everyone is

going to."

"I believe him," James said quietly.

"And so do I," Jessica added. She was standing close to James, looking across the large dining table at Greg and the minister standing by the marble fireplace.

Mr. Peterson nodded. "Well, that's something, I can't keep you here all night, Greg. You have to go home straight away. I'll get properly dressed and we'll see what we can do. We should have some news of Brian soon. My wife is with him at the hospital tonight."

He went upstairs, leaving the three of them in silence in the dining room.

After a time Greg said, "I wonder what will happen now."

Again there was silence. James wondered what they could say that would help. Anyway, what did the minister have in mind? There was the sound of a car stopping outside. Greg looked frightened again.

"Who's that?" he asked. "It's the police, I know it is!"

"Don't worry," James said. "Mr. Peterson will speak up for you."

Someone was in the hall now. The door to their room opened slowly.

"Is that you, John? I've just——. Oh!" Mrs. Peterson stood there in her coat, with a green scarf on her head. “What are you all doing here?” she asked in surprise.

“It’s about Brian,” James said, getting to his feet.

At that moment, Mr. Peterson appeared, now fully dressed. He explained to his wife the reason for the visitors in the middle of the night.

“I’ve just come from the hospital,” Mrs. Peterson said. “Brian’s mother wanted me to go and see him.”

“How is he?” Greg asked, sounding genuinely concerned.

“He’d only just come round when I left.”

“Just come round?” Greg asked.

“From the operation. A large splinter from the tree was lodged in his neck.”

“Is he all right, Mrs. Peterson?”

Mrs. Peterson nodded. “Yes, Greg, as well as can be expected.”

Greg looked at the floor. “Will he ... will he ... live?” he asked awkwardly.

“Oh yes, he’ll live,” Mrs. Peterson said more brightly. “I meant he wasn’t very comfortable. It was hurting him a lot. He’ll be in for a few days, but he’d in no danger now.”

James noticed a sudden change in the atmosphere. It was as though the sun had come out on a cold and rainy day.

The minister looked thoughtful. “We’ll not be

able to see Brian's mother tonight if she's still at the hospital. We'll have to wait for the morning."

"We?" Greg was looking very tired.

Mr. Peterson took Greg by the arm.

"What about my dad?" Greg asked as he let himself be led from the room.

"That's where we're both going now," Mr. Peterson explained kindly.

"No, I'd rather not." Greg tried to pull away.

"Come on." Mr. Peterson opened the front door. "You have to go back some time. Your parents are worried enough as it is. The longer you leave it, the worse it will be for them – and for you!"

Greg nodded. "Well ... okay." He sounded far from convinced. He walked slowly from the safety of the vicarage. In the drive he paused and turned. "Thanks for coming down with me," he said to the Two Jays.

James said, "Perhaps we'll see you tomorrow."

Greg shook his head. "I dunno," he muttered. "It all depends."

"He's going to be in serious trouble with his father," Mrs. Peterson said as soon as Greg was gone.

"I thought you said his father wanted him to be tough," Jessica said.

"Yes, tough, but his father thinks he was a coward to run off like that."

"Does he think Greg hurt Brian on purpose?"

James asked.

Mrs. Peterson smiled a tired smile. “I shouldn’t think the idea has even entered his head. Take my advice and don’t even mention it – if you ever have the misfortune to meet him.”

“But *I* don’t think Greg did anything to Brian. I think it was an accident exactly as Greg said. Don’t you?”

Mrs. Peterson stayed silent for a moment. “Perhaps,” she said at last. “Yes, perhaps it was an accident. I don’t think Brian is trying to cover up for his friend.” She sighed slowly. “Maybe we’ll never know. One thing *is* certain, I wouldn’t like to be in Greg’s shoes when he gets home. I think *my husband* is brave enough to be going there! I’m afraid poor Greg is going to be the subject of quite a bit of nasty gossip in this village for a while.”

James gave a loud yawn he was unable to cover up.

Mrs. Peterson smiled. “I’ll walk back to the cottage with you. James, if your parents want to know what’s been going on, one of us will come round in the morning and explain. I think perhaps we’ll let them stay sleeping for the rest of the night. They wouldn’t thank me for waking them up at half past one!”

Chapter Nine

AN OLD LETTER

Once again it was knocking at the door that woke James. This time the room was light. He looked at his phone. It was nearly ... *ten o'clock*!

"I'll go!" a loud shout came from Jessica, and James heard her come down the stairs in great jumps. Then James heard his parents talking in the kitchen. Everyone else was up!

He pushed his hair back and staggered out of his make-shift bed on the sofa. It must have been comfortable after all, in spite of the gap between the cushions that was in the wrong place. Jessica was talking to someone. He pushed his head round the door and peered into the hallway.

"It's Mr. Peterson," Jessica said. "He's come to tell us about Brian. Hey, you look half dead. We thought you were never going to wake up."

The minister was in the narrow hallway with James's parents. He smiled at James.

"I've called in to give you the latest news about Brian Tucker. You'll be glad to know he's completely out of danger. He'll be in hospital for a few days yet. I've got Greg Hawker in the car outside, so I won't stay. We're on our way to the hospital to visit Brian."

"Can we go with you?" Jessica asked. "We'd like to see how he is."

"I don't think so," Mr. Peterson said. Then he added quickly, "I'm sure you'll be able to visit at some time. It's just that I expect Greg would rather be on his own. I'll ask him if you like."

"No," James said. After all, there was no point in making things difficult for Greg. He was in enough trouble as it was.

"It's all right, you can if you wants to." It was Greg, leaning against the doorway. He must have got tired of waiting and come to see what was happening.

"Thanks all the same," James said, "but we can go another day."

Greg shook his head. "You did a lot to help him. I expect he'd like to see you both."

"Then you don't mind if we come with you?" James asked.

"Mind? No, not if there's room in the car." Greg turned to Mr. Peterson. "Is it all right?"

The young minister turned to James's parents. "If it's all right with you, Mr. and Mrs. Cooper. We seem to have decided this on our own!"

Mrs. Cooper laughed. "Quite all right. Jessica's been telling us about the adventure last night."

Mr. Peterson nodded. "James and Jessica did

well to help Greg like that. However, I have two or three people to visit when I'm in town. It might be better if they came back on the bus. Greg will know which one. It would save them waiting around for me and getting fed up."

Mrs. Cooper turned to James and Jessica, and opened her purse. "Here's some money for the bus, James. Come straight back when you've been to the hospital."

James smiled. Greg would be with them on the bus back to Sheppingford. He was never too happy when travelling on a strange bus route for the first time.

Mr. Peterson and Greg waited in the cottage for James to get dressed and have a hurried breakfast of a glass of milk, and a round of bread and butter with marmalade. He noticed there was now a spoon in the marmalade jar, which took the fun out of it a bit.

"That should keep me going until lunchtime," he explained, wiping his mouth with a paper towel.

The car soon left the village of Sheppingford behind. James and Jessica sat in the back, each trying to tell their latest ideas on the poisoned animals, Saint Cerig, the stone heads, and anything else they could think of.

Suddenly James remembered his idea of using a dye to trace the water supply. Greg, coming in the middle of the night had put it completely from his mind. He mentioned his theory that the poison was coming from the quarry, and everyone listened with obvious interest as he explained his idea for using dye.

"My mum tried blue dye in cake icing once," Jessica said. "Only a few drops and the icing went bright blue. Everyone scraped the icing off before eating the cake. She never did it again!"

Mr. Peterson shook his head. "You can't just use any sort of dye. You might go poisoning more of the animals yourself. There's a special dye that cavers use to trace water, but I don't think you'd be able to get hold of it. It turns the water a sort of green, and anyone irresponsible could make a nuisance of themselves with it."

"But *we* wouldn't make a nuisance of ourselves," James promised. "We'd just use it sensibly. All we want to do is to see if the tiny stream in the quarry comes out in any of the wells."

The minister looked thoughtful. "Yes, I understand why you want to help. I'll tell you what. I know someone who's a very keen cave explorer on the Mendips. A speleologist. Some call them potholers. It's possible I might be able to get hold of a small amount of the dye he uses. But if I can't, I want you to promise me you won't go putting any sort of dye in the water. You might do a lot of damage, even though you wouldn't mean to."

Everyone promised. What Mr. Peterson said

was really only commonsense, but in their excitement James thought perhaps they might have rushed ahead and done something stupid.

"Right now, here's the hospital. If I drop you off by the main gate, you can make your own way in. I'll call and see Brian this afternoon, and see you back in Sheppingford later."

"Goodbye," Jessica called, "and thank you. I hope you can get hold of some proper dye!"

The hospital was not at all as James had pictured it was going to be. His local hospital was new, but this one was an old Victorian building.

"This way," a nurse said, leading them along a corridor where the floor and paintwork looked shiny and clean. "He's in the children's ward."

James was aware of a strong smell of something, probably antiseptic in the air. He took a long sniff and found it rather unpleasant. It reminded him of a short stay he'd once had in hospital when his tonsils were removed.

The nurse opened one half of a double door leading to a long ward filled with beds. Most of the children were either walking about, or sitting round a table playing games or making Lego models. Others were watching the TV. Very few were in bed. There was no sign of Brian.

"He's at the far end," the nurse explained. "He has to stay in bed. We expect to have him up for a few minutes tomorrow."

All eyes were now turned on them. Except Brian's. There was still no sign of Brian. The nurse went over to a bed that was certainly occupied. They could tell that from the hump under the white hospital blanket. The nurse lifted it back.

"Go away!"

"Brian, you've got some visitors."

"Don't want them!"

"Well, I can't make you see them." The nurse turned to Jessica and James and smiled.

"Put these by his bed," Greg told her, looking slightly embarrassed. He handed the nurse a bag of liquorice allsorts and a packet of popcorn he'd brought with him. The bag made a rustling sound.

A sudden change came over the hump in the bed. "It's you!" he said, sitting up slowly. Then he noticed James and Jessica. "What did you bring *them* for?"

"At least you're welcome!" the nurse said quietly, with a wink to Jessica. "I'll leave you for a few minutes, but you'd better not stay long." She moved away to settle an argument that had broken out between two children sitting at the table.

"How's you?" Greg asked, after a long silence.

Brian settled down in the bed again. "All right. Hurts a bit when I moves my head." He pointed to a large dressing on his neck.

"Have they asked you any questions?" Greg pulled up a chair so he could sit by the side of the bed. “Here, have one.” He helped himself to a liquorice allsort and handed the bag to Brian who pushed it away.

Brian frowned. “What about?”

“About how it happened, young ’un.”

“Only the doctor. No police or nothing like that.” Brian sounded very West Country.

Greg looked relieved. He helped himself to another sweet. “What did you say?”

“I just told them how it happened.”

“How?”

“Just what happened.” Brian pulled the thin blanket round himself.

Greg sounded anxious. “How *did* it happen?” he demanded.

Brian giggled. “Don’t you remember?”

“Of course I do. All I wants to know is how *you* said it happened.”

“You’ll soon find out,” Brian said, and he retreated even further under the blanket.

Greg got to his feet. He clenched his fists. “I’ve got to know!”

Brian was silent this time, but he sneaked a look out from under the bedding. Greg put his head close. “You ought to be glad you’re still alive. I’ve been praying for you!”

Brian sat up in bed again, and Jessica and James stared in surprise.

“You?” Brian said. *“You?”* He sounded almost

scornful, but it might have been surprise. "Why would *you* pray?"

"You were glad of it, when you was lying on the hill," Greg retorted, sounding quite worked up.

"That were different. I'm all right now, ain't I? Well then, I don't need to bother praying no more."

"You said you'd try and be a proper Christian," Greg reminded him.

"You make me sick!" Brian said.

The nurse, probably attracted by the raised voices, came over. "You mustn't get him excited," she explained. "I think perhaps you'd better be going. Why not call in again tomorrow?"

"I don't think I'll bother," Greg said miserably.

James felt upset by the whole affair. The only remarkable thing seemed to be Greg's change of ideas about praying. They were escorted down the corridor, and from there they made their own way out through the front door.

The hospital grounds looked attractive, and were a lot quieter than the ward they'd just left. The smell of the flowers was better than the smell of the hospital. James bent over to examine shiny flat insects like wasps that hovered near the flowerbeds.

"We might as well get the bus back to Sheppingford," Greg says gloomily. "I don't know why we bothered to come!"

"Perhaps his neck hurts a lot," Jessica suggested.

Greg shrugged, and took a powerful kick at a stone in the drive, sending it shooting out through the main gates. "I don't know what he's told them about the accident," he muttered.

"It *was* an accident, wasn't it?" James asked.

Greg swung round, and James wished he'd kept quiet. "Don't you believe me, then?"

"I think so," James said, but he wasn't really sure what to think anymore.

Greg narrowed his eyes slightly. "You'd better, boy, you'd better!"

Greg started to cheer up when they were out of the hospital grounds. "Let's go and get some lunch," he suggested after he'd examined the timetable on the bus shelter. "The bus won't be here for nearly an hour."

James spotted a cafe near the bus stop and he suddenly began to feel extraordinarily hungry. He'd not had any real breakfast, and probably Jessica hadn't either. He felt in his pocket and his face showed disappointment. "You go if you like. I'll stay out here with Jessica and keep a lookout for the bus. It might come early."

"Short of money?" Greg asked, in a kinder voice than normal.

"Just a little," James confessed. "I've only got the money for the bus."

Jessica dug deep in the pocket of her jeans. "I've probably got enough."

Greg, who was bigger and older than either of the Two Jays, gave one of his rare laughs. "I'll buy you something. After all, I did ask you to come with me."

James felt pleased with the offer. He looked at the menu on the board outside and decided to make it a cheap meal. Anyway, sausages, baked beans and chips bought out were a great treat!

"I've always been interested in Saint Cerig," Greg said suddenly, looking up from his large burger. "Ever since I were a nipper. My gran gave I an old letter from him once."

"Letter?" Jessica asked. "What sort of letter?"

Greg shook his head. "I dunno. It's all in foreign."

"Can we see it?" James asked with interest. It sounded exciting and mysterious.

They were unable to get any more information from Greg, and ate their meal planning how to use the dye – if Mr. Peterson could get some.

When they arrived back in Sheppingford, James asked Greg again about the letter "all in foreign."

"I'll bring it round to your cottage," he offered.

James would have been happy with the offer, but Jessica was impatient. "Can't we come round for it now?" she asked.

Greg looked doubtful. "Best not. My dad might be in."

Jessica nodded. "That's all right. We'll wait

outside while you go in. You might forget otherwise."

James was unable to see what difference it made whether Greg's father was home or not. He looked around. There were a lot of houses where Greg lived. He and Jessica waited outside while Greg went in to get the old letter.

Greg's garden was untidy. Dirty curtains hung at the front window. Suddenly there was a shout. A large man stood by the front door. "Go on, clear off! I'm not having no son of mine bringing shame on this house."

James peeped through the hedge and noticed the peeling wallpaper inside the front door. He wondered whether Greg's father – it must be his father – cared much about anything anyway. Greg shot out of the house holding a book. He looked angry.

"Don't take no notice of him," he muttered. "Come on, let's go to your place."

James's parents were in the small back yard. They asked how Brian was getting on, and then changed the subject so as not to embarrass Greg.

James's father pointed up the stairs. "I've got good news. The owner of the cottage came today and suggested we move out and either go home or find other accommodation in the area," he said.

"And that's good news?" Jessica asked.

James gave a groan. "Sounds like bad news."

"You can blame me," Mrs. Cooper said.

"Oh, Mum, no, we're staying put," James said. "That sofa is *ever* so comfy."

His mother laughed. "I didn't say what you can blame me for. You can blame me for making you sleep on the sofa for the rest of the holiday!"

"Does that mean we're staying?" James asked, frowning. He felt muddled.

His mother laughed. "I told the owner there's absolutely *no* way we're leaving here. So he's covered over the damaged slates to keep the rain out, but he can't mend the ceiling in your little bedroom, James, until it dries out."

"Oh, Aunty Amy, you're so lovely." Jessica came round and gave her a big hug. "Are you sure you don't mind?"

Mrs. Cooper laughed. "I have to admit when I first saw this cottage I thought we were in for the worst holiday ever. Now I've come to love it, so please don't feel sorry for me. This is a family holiday, and we want everyone to enjoy it."

Once the excitement was over, James's father noticed the book Greg was holding. "Is that something interesting?" he asked.

Greg explained that the book was very old, with engravings of West Country scenes. There wasn't much about this area, but tucked inside the back cover was a very old piece of paper.

Greg said he had no idea where it had come

from, but his grandmother had given him the book when he was small, because he liked looking at the pictures. She was now dead – "Dead for many a long year."

Mr. Cooper took the old document. "It's in Latin," he remarked. "I used to learn Latin at school. For some reason I found it quite easy. Let's see. Yes, it's certainly about someone called Cerig."

"I knows that," Greg said proudly. "Cerigus is the first word, so I sort of guessed it were Cerig."

James's father sighed. "Oh dear, I never thought I'd be translating Latin again. Ah, here's a word I know. *Vi* – by force. Some of the words are starting to come back to me. Yes, 'I was taken by force.' It's no good, I'd need a Latin dictionary to translate this little lot."

James groaned in despair. They were surely so close to a great discovery, and now they would never know what it said. "Who's going to have a Latin dictionary in Sheppingford?" he asked.

His father looked brighter. "Perhaps Mr. Peterson would have one. Run and ask him, James."

Jessica picked up her phone. "Stay here. I can download one if I go outside."

While Jessica went into the garden to get a signal on her phone, James examined the document. It was old, but clearly not nearly as old as Saint Cerig, because it was written on paper, not vellum. It was either a copy of one of his writings, or something that had been written about him. The ink had faded to a pale brown in places, and some of the words were difficult to read where they ran along folds in the page.

While Mr. Cooper was copying out the Latin sentences as well as he could, ready for making the translation, there was a knock on the door. Mr. Peterson stood there.

"I have good news about the dye," he announced. "My friend Philip Everett from the caving group is willing to help."

"Do you have the dye with you?" James asked, feeling excited.

Mr. Peterson shook his head. "It is not as simple as that. It needs to be done by an expert, or you can get very misleading results."

"So...." James said no more and shook his head sadly.

The minister laughed. "Don't worry, James. Philip will come here tomorrow morning and you can explain your theory about the mineshaft to him. And he might have some helpful advice to give. Don't you worry, if you think there's water getting from the old mineshaft into what you call Saint Cerig's well, he'll be able to prove it — one way or the other."

James tried not to let his disappointment show. Experts? Who needed experts? All anyone had to do was to put some dye down the mineshaft and see if the water in the well turned green or brown or blue, or whatever colour it was supposed to turn.

The minister said he had to be getting back, but wanted them to let him know what the document was all about. With the aid of the downloaded dictionary, James's father was able to complete the translation. He had to copy the translation out again, because the first attempt was full of corrections.

"Here you are. I think we've got the general meaning. Mind you, it may not be very accurate." He sighed. "The problem isn't so much in translating the Latin, as in reading the Latin words in the first place. The writing is really bad. I very much doubt the person who copied this from the original could speak Latin, which is why they seem to have made lots of mistakes. It seems to me to be a letter written by Saint Cerig."

He read it out to the three eager listeners. "Cerigus, servant of our Lord, to the godly man of **XXXXXXXXX**, greetings." (The name of the place had been badly smudged, and was right along one of the folds.)

"The time has come for me to go to my Lord and Saviour. Last night my habitation was invaded by savages. In my own habitation I am captive. Even now, dear friend, I await death. They have already looted the house of God and are determined I shall not live. Take care of my head, although they have betrayed me. Remove them to safety. They cannot read this letter."

"Take care of my head?" Jessica repeated with a shudder. "That sounds horrible. I know they did nasty things in those days, but are you sure that bit's right, Uncle Clive?"

Mr. Cooper looked again. "Heads, that should be — not head. Remove *them* to safety."

"Then what does he mean about the heads reading?" James asked. "Heads can't read — unless they're joined to bodies!"

His father shook his head. "I suppose he meant the savages couldn't read. It's a bit confusing."

Greg wasn't sharing the excitement of the others. "Savages? There ain't no savages in Sheppingford — never was, I shouldn't think! It's nothing to do with *our* Saint Cerig."

Mr. Cooper picked up the original letter again. "Oh, I think it is. Savages is just my translation. Ruffians or gangsters might be a better word."

"Poor old Saint Cerig," Jessica said quietly. "I wonder if they did kill him."

James was frowning. "I wonder how the heads gave him away — or what they were." He felt excited now, and he and Jessica told of their discovery with the pattern on the smooth rock face by the well — and the stones under the mud and leaves. Perhaps there were enough there to have been the foundations for Saint Cerig's chapel.

Mrs. Cooper looked into the front room. "I'm getting tea ready for you," she said, "so don't go rushing off just yet."

Greg got up to leave.

"No, you stay as well, Greg. I'm getting it ready for everyone. I'm sure you're as hungry as all the others. Besides, you know a lot about Sheppingford and all round here. You can tell us where we can have some interesting walks."

Greg was quiet at first during the meal, but eventually he became more talkative. He seemed to realise he could be very useful in sharing his local knowledge.

Jessica reached for the biscuit tin. "Any chocolate biscuits left, Aunty Amy?"

Mrs. Cooper nodded. "Be careful, though. Make sure there aren't any creepy-crawlies in there. I found a large earwig in the cornflakes this morning."

"Ugh!" Jessica said. "Not in mine, I hope."

Mrs. Cooper laughed. "In the packet."

Jessica began to look quite pale. "Was that before or after I had mine?"

"Before. But I got it out. I'm sure you didn't eat it."

Jessica pushed her plate away. "How disgusting! How horribly disgusting! If I'd known that, I wouldn't have had *any* cornflakes."

Mrs. Cooper smiled. “That’s why I didn’t say anything at the time. Don’t worry, you’re none the worse for it.”

Jessica screwed her face up. “I’ve gone off my food. I’m not having anything else, thanks.”

“Good,” James said, reaching for the tin. “I’ll have your biscuit, and my own. A few earwigs won’t hurt *me*.” In spite of what he said, he felt slightly off his food as well. There was one good thing in all this. His mother would probably have insisted on going home if earwigs and a collapsed ceiling had happened on their first day!

After they’d eaten, a lot of yawning went on from James and Jessica, and Greg dropped off to sleep on James’s sofa.

Mrs. Cooper said to let Greg sleep for a bit longer, and later on Mr. Cooper rather bravely took him home in the car. He came back to say that he had no idea what had gone on in Greg’s house, but there had been a lot of shouting.

<><><>

Soon after breakfast the next morning they heard a car stop outside, followed by a knock on the door. A tall man with a large bushy beard stood there. “I think I’ve got the right place,” he said “I’m here to help trace a water supply using dye.”

“Come in, come in,” James called. “We’ll tell you all about it.”

The visitor, who introduced himself as Philip

Everett, had a backpack in one hand. He came in and was shown into the small kitchen. He was so tall he had to duck his head to go through the doorway. Sitting at the kitchen table he looked enormous, and James wondered how someone this large could ever squeeze through the narrow passages in the Mendip caves. But he kept quiet.

Between them, Jessica and James explained their theory that pollution in the mineshaft could be getting through to the pool of water that they were calling the real Saint Cerig's well, but not to any of the other wells and springs.

It didn't take long for Philip Everett to understand their concern about Farmer Osborne's animals being poisoned in that field, and only in that field.

"I'll call and see Farmer Osborne," he said, "and have a word with him and explain what we're doing. The dye is completely harmless and invisible."

"Invisible?" James asked. "What's the point of using invisible dye?"

"Invisible in daylight," Philip Everett said. "Do you know what ultraviolet light is?"

James nodded. "It's what gives you sunburn."

Philip Everett opened his backpack and removed what looked like a large flashlight. "This is an ultraviolet light source." He pointed it at Jessica's T-shirt, turning it bright blue where the beam shone.

"Wow," was all James could say.

Philip Everett nodded. "Impressive, eh?"

"And you shine is on the dye in the water, and it glows bright blue." Jessica was catching on fast.

"You're right, except this dye glows bright green. But it's not as simple as that, and it needs an expert to use it. You show me where the mineshaft is, but don't go anywhere near there once I've used the dye."

"It's perfectly safe," James insisted. "It's full almost to the top."

Philip Everett shook his head. "That's not the problem. This dye is a powder that I mix with the water. If you get even the slightest trace of dye on your shoes or your hands, you might go down to the well and contaminate the water yourselves. And that, of course, would give a completely misleading result."

Jessica looked excited. "So you put some dye down the mineshaft, while we're waiting at the well with your magic light waiting for the water to shine bright green? Is that right?"

"Tomorrow. You check the well tomorrow."

"But tomorrow might be too late?" James protested. "The water and the dye might have gone through and we'll miss it."

Philip Everett produced a sealed bag from his backpack. "This is a special fibre," he explained, sounding remarkably patient. "It acts as a filter. We go to the well first, before I touch the dye, and place some filters there. The dye clings to the fibres, and over the next two or three days we can check to see if the dye is caught there. If it is, it will fluoresce bright green."

With great excitement, Jessica and James took Philip Everett to the old quarry. The expert caver said he would have to mix the dye with water to feed it into the small stream that was running over the edge of the mineshaft.

"There was much more water yesterday," Jessica said. "Does it matter?"

Philip Everett shook his head. "If this water comes out at your well, we'll know for sure, no matter how much water is running here. I've been thinking about the dead sheep. If it was a dry time, there would be very little water running down the mineshaft, if any water at all. So any chemical liquid tipped down here would be very concentrated when it reached the well. It's such a stupid and dangerous thing to do, dumping chemicals like that."

Greg turned up as they were making their way down to the well. Jessica explained what they were doing, and Greg seemed to catch on quickly.

"So we waits by the well for the green water," he said.

Philip Everett explained to Greg that the water didn't really turn green. Not green enough to show up with the ultra violet light.

"We use these," he said, and produced three small net bags from his backpack and hung them on wire frames in the water. Then he did the same in the depression that the locals believed to be the real Saint Cerig's well. He explained that the fibres in the filters would catch the dye, and it would stay there for a day or more, depending on the flow of the water.

Philip Everett left them the ultraviolet light so they could check the filters morning and evening over the next few days.

James gave a groan. "Days?"

The caving expert laughed. "Maybe tomorrow if you're lucky. And don't forget to check the well in the middle of the field. And keep away from the quarry in case there's any dye on the ground up there."

He explained he wouldn't come down to the well again, in case he contaminated the ground with his feet. Then he made his way alone back up to the mineshaft in the old quarry.

Chapter Ten

GREG'S GREAT DISCOVERY

At seven o'clock the next morning, Greg was already waiting at the well.

"Hurry up and let's see if it's worked!" he shouted as he saw Jessica and James coming across the field. "I've been waiting here for ages. My dad threw me out of the house."

The well was in the shade, and Greg lifted the first filter from the wire where it was hanging in the water. Jessica and James crowded close to make sure it was even more shaded from the daylight, and Jessica switched on the ultraviolet lamp.

Absolutely nothing showed green on the fibres. No matter how much they put the filters in the shade – zero.

They tried the "proper" Saint Cerig's well in the middle of the field, and again there was no sign of anything green on the filters.

"It's nothing but rubbish," Greg protested. "We'm wasting our time."

"I think we're just too impatient," Jessica said calmly. "We'll come back this evening as soon as it's dark. The water might take ages to get here from the mineshaft. If there's any dye on the filters, Philip Everett said it won't wash away immediately. Come on, Greg, cheer up. I still think we're onto something important."

<><><>

"Look at that!" James said that evening. "It can't be anything else but the dye, can it?"

"It has to be," Jessica said. "We checked the filters when we put them in yesterday, and there was nothing on them, and there was nothing on them this morning. I can see why Philip Everett was so fussy about us not going near the old quarry, and why he didn't come here after he put the dye down the mineshaft. This has to be one hundred percent proof that the water in the mineshaft flows through here."

"It's all that muck and rubbish filling the shaft," James said. "It *must* be something to do with that man at the quarry. What was his name? Mr. Slade, wasn't it? I *thought* he was up to no good. He wouldn't have chased us away like that if he wasn't trying to hide something. Perhaps he had a big argument with Farmer Osborne, and he's doing it out of spite."

"Mr. Slade ought to be locked away," Greg muttered in disgust. "I likes Farmer Osborne, and I feels sorry for him."

"Let's go and tell my dad," James suggested. "He'll know what to do."

"Wait a moment," Jessica said. "We've not checked the filters we put in the well in the middle of the field."

Greg shook his head. "Waste of time," he said. "They're going to be green too."

But they weren't. No matter how carefully they shone the ultraviolet light on the filters, they stayed dark.

"Well, there's a mystery," James said. He realised what he'd just said, but the others didn't seem to get the unintended joke. He tried again. "Well, well, well, there's a mystery." But no one seemed to hear.

"Come on," Jessica urged. "It's time to make our report."

The three arrived breathless at the cottage. It was some time before they could tell their tale.

James's father looked concerned. "Let's see if we can have a word with Mr. Slade, the quarry man tomorrow morning. It might save a lot of unpleasantness. Have you considered he might have a perfectly good explanation for wanting to keep you out of his quarry?"

"It isn't *his* quarry anyway," Jessica protested. "Farmer Osborne says *anyone* in the village can go there and get stone."

James's father nodded. "Yes, and anybody can go there and tip poison down the mineshaft – if that's where the poison is coming from."

"Aren't you going to the police?" James asked, afraid his father wasn't treating their discovery with any urgency.

"Of course the police will have to be informed. This is a very serious matter. You've made an important discovery – or rather, you *seem* to have made one. I know," he added quickly, before James could interrupt, "I know your *tests* show that the quarry is the source of the poison, but the water in the quarry stream must come from somewhere. It might have already been poisoned before it got there. We don't want to go stirring up trouble by accusing people without proof."

This was something James hadn't thought about. They'd been *so* sure the poison had come directly from the mineshaft.

"Cheer up," his father said. "You seem to have discovered where the underground stream runs, and it only goes to one of the wells. There must be some very unexpected water channels under the ground. You've done most of the work in solving this riddle. Now, there is one thing I'd like to do this evening. I'd like to come down and see the pattern you've found on the rock face."

"What, now?" James looked out of the small kitchen window. "It's dark!"

"That's good. We'll need the gas lanterns. It will be a bit of an adventure. We'll call and see Mr. Peterson on the way, and ask him if he's got any chalk. His wife might use it in her Discoverers group."

"Chalk? Come on, Dad, you're pulling our legs!"

Greg looked happy and a little surprised to hear the family joking together. James was now glad they'd met him.

Mr. Peterson' wife had a box of white chalk, and she and her husband asked if they also could have a look at the discovery of the pattern.

With James's mother there were seven of them. The Petersons had each brought powerful LED flashlights, and with the two gas lanterns from the cottage they looked like a party of carol singers – out of season!

James was leading the way into the trees when he suddenly froze. Someone — or something — was moving close to the rock. He felt a push in his back.

Jessica squeezed past. "Ah, good," she said. "There's my fleece, hanging on that bush. I was wondering where I'd left it!"

"Show us the pattern," Mr. Cooper said quickly, as though he'd also been jumpy and wanted a change the subject to cover up his embarrassment.

Jessica pointed to the rock face and then let out a cry. "Hey, look how easy it is to see the lines now! It looks as though they've been cut deeper. Why is that, Uncle Clive?"

James's father picked up his lantern. "Ah, that's why I wanted to come here after dark. When the light from one of the lanterns shines across the rock, the lines are in shadow. They stand out more from the light grey colour of the rock. When I bring my light round to the front like this ... see ... they almost disappear."

Jessica had brought the ultraviolet light source with her, and demonstrated how the filters in the water still showed patches of bright green. She was anxious that the adults should be convinced of the results of the dye test.

After everyone had looked, and sounded impressed, Mr. Cooper opened the box of chalk and asked for just one of the lanterns. James was keen to find out what the chalk was for.

"Now then, stand well back. I don't want any other lights shining on here. James and Jessica, you can help me. I'll stand to one side with this lantern, and I want you to chalk inside all the lines that are in shadow."

The plan was now obvious. So obvious that James felt he ought to have thought of it himself. Anyway, he hadn't, but he and Jessica could make a good job of filling in the lines. What was the picture of? He couldn't tell yet. Perhaps when he stood back a bit....

"It's an angel!" Greg shouted loudly, making everyone jump. "It's one of God's angels!"

All the lights shone onto the chalk picture that was taking shape, and sure enough Greg was right.

The chalking continued until all the lines were filled in. Mr. Peterson explained what he thought the whole picture showed.

"This side looks like Adam and Eve being tempted by the devil in the form of a serpent." He pointed to the shapes that had now come to mean something. "Over here we seem to have an angel blowing a trumpet. It's very crudely done. I think one side is meant to show the beginning of man when sin first came into the world, and this side shows the end of the world when those who are in God's family will go to heaven to live for ever."

"I like it," James said after a silence. "I don't suppose Saint Cerig used chalk."

"Paint, I expect," Mr. Peterson said. "He lived in the time when the churches were brightly painted inside. The walls, the pillars, everything that people could get a paint brush to."

"Like the painting of Saint Cerig in the church?" James asked.

"Yes, but the decorations were brighter. Then in the Reformation everything was painted white, but in some old churches the white paint has now been removed, leaving large mediaeval pictures on the wall."

"Why paint pictures all over the walls?" Jessica asked. "I thought it was just the occasional wall painting like yours. It seems all wrong."

"It was in the time when only a few people could

read. The pictures often illustrated scenes from the Bible, and people could look at them every week, or even every day, and see the Bible stories for themselves. And most important of all, the pictures would help them remember what they were being taught."

James laughed. "Like a comic strip," he said aloud, then realised he was probably right.

"Exactly," Mr. Peterson said. "And the only copies of the Bible at the time were in Latin, so only highly educated people could read it."

Jessica looked thoughtful. "So people would have come here, and Saint Cerrig pointed to the pictures on the wall and taught them God's Word from the Bible – speaking in English," she said. "It's amazing, but I'm glad I didn't live in mediaeval times. They didn't have mobile phones or computers back then."

"That was the least of their problems," Mr. Peterson said, smiling at Jessica's statement. "They had diseases like bubonic plague and the black death. People died very young. No modern medicines and hospitals. They were certainly hard times in which to live."

"So why was he a saint?" James asked. "I've only just thought of that."

Mr. Peterson took a deep breath. "You're a saint, too," he said to James. "And so are you, Jessica."

James shook his head. "I don't think you're right." He laughed an embarrassed laugh. "I don't think I'm a *saint*."

"Didn't you know that in the New Testament all Christians are called saints? The Epistles were written to the saints in the churches – in other words to all the Christians."

"So Saint Cerig wasn't anyone special?" James said, feeling rather stunned by the thought that he was also a saint.

"Everyone is special in God's eyes," Mr. Peterson said, "but some people tend to think of people like Saint Cerig being more holy than others. We know very little about him, except that's the title he got stuck with."

"Wow," James said. "What do you think of that, Saint Jessica?"

Jessica agreed that the letters to the churches in the New Testament were written to the saints in the churches, so Mr. Peterson must be right.

"Check it out for yourself," Mr. Peterson said. "Many people think that to be a saint you have to have worked some special miracle, but that's not so, although some folk do seem to be more godly than others."

"So I really *am* a saint," James said.

"Don't let it go to your head, James," Jessica told him. "You're a saint in God's eyes, not mine!"

James nodded. "I'll go along with that."

Jessica ran her fingers of the rock face. “Do you really think this wall was painted in bright colours?” she asked.

“Most probably,” Mr. Peterson said. “Of course, the paint would have washed off a long time ago. It’s likely Saint Cerig had a handwritten copy of the Bible, or maybe just the four Gospels. They were written on animal skin, which we call vellum. This was before the days of printing, and Bibles were copied by hand by monks living in monasteries.”

They turned to the pile of stones. James looked disappointed. “There aren’t nearly enough here to build a chapel.”

“Build a chapel?” Greg asked “You ain’t thinking of building one, are ’ee!”

James shook his head. “Not likely! But if there were never any more stones than this, neither could Saint Cerig.” He stood back and wiped his hands on his jeans. Had the saint really been killed here? Was this where the letter had been written? The *letter*! What had it said about heads? *Heads!* Of course. How silly not to have thought of it before. The mysterious heads in the village church. They must be the same ones! *“Those two heads belong in the two holes in the rock!”* he shouted in excitement.

Jessica let out a squeal of delight, and then sighed deeply. “Maybe now they’ve been taken away from here, we’ll never be able to see how they ‘betrayed’ Saint Cerig, as the old letter said.”

"Perhaps we can find out though," James said excitedly. "There's no knowing what we can do if we try hard enough."

<><><>

The next morning, as he'd promised, James's father went round to find Mr. Slade. It was Saturday, so the quarry was deserted, but he found him at his home in the village. When he got back, he explained what had happened.

"I'm pretty sure Mr. Slade had nothing to do with it. He seems such a pleasant man. I can't think why he chased you away like he did."

"Perhaps he was just tricking you," a suspicious James suggested.

His father smiled. "No, I'm sure he was telling me the truth."

"But, Uncle Clive, Greg says *he's* telling the truth about Brian's accident," Jessica protested. "Hardly anyone seems to believe *him*."

Mr. Cooper nodded. "That's quite true, but I didn't say *I* believed Greg."

James was surprised. "Do you think he's lying?"

"Greg? I just don't know what to make of his story, but I'm sure Mr. Slade from the quarry *is* telling the truth. Anyway, I'm going to see the police and explain about your discovery that the water's coming from the old mineshaft. Mr. Slade has had his chance to tell me if he's responsible for it. Perhaps you'd better both come with me. It was your idea to use dye to trace the water."

This meant another car journey, but Jessica and James were keen to explain their ideas to the police. They felt they'd done well to track down where the water in the well came from.

The police were clearly interested, even though it was a Saturday. No reports of poisoned animals had come in for several days in the village of Sheppingford. It was quite obvious to Mr. Cooper and the Two Jays that they weren't going to start any new investigations until Monday. They already knew about Mr. Slade working the quarry. They, too, thought it unlikely he was to blame.

"At the moment it looks as though one of the farmers – I won't name any names – was careless with some highly toxic brushwood killer. Maybe accidentally. Who knows? He'd hardly admit to it, would he! Especially if he's caused the death of another farmer's animals. Just because the water in the well comes from the quarry, it doesn't prove that the poison was in the well." With that, the interview was over.

Outside the police station James was hopping mad. "All that hard work and they couldn't care less!"

"Cool down," his father advised him. "They didn't say you'd wasted their time. They'll report it on Monday morning to one of the senior officers, and he'll decide what to do. You can't expect them to discuss it with you."

James could see the sense of this, but for the rest of the day, as he and Jessica cleared the area around the well, he kept feeling extremely cross.

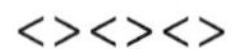

After an early lunch James and Jessica returned to the well. In a moment of panic James remembered the dead rabbit he'd earlier covered with leaves. It had gone. Maybe a fox had taken it. Whatever had had happened to it, it wouldn't be upsetting Jessica. And so far, no other animas had turned up dead or seriously ill.

Using the old spade from the cottage, they dug the leaves and soil from around the "foundations." There were certainly enough stones deep in the ground for the chapel to have been built on. There was even a gap that could have been for a doorway opposite the rock face, but they were surprised by how small the building must have been.

"Hardly room to lie down," Jessica said.

"Perhaps he was a tiny saint," James added with a smile.

"We went down to Cornwell last year," Jessica said. "Remember how nearly every place seemed to be Saint this or Saint that?"

James said he remembered the names. "Dad says most of them would have been early missionaries. They came hundreds of years ago to tell people in the towns and villages about Jesus. I think there were some who were just hermits who lived alone. It's a shame no one knows anything about Saint Cerig."

"I'm sure he was a godly man," Jessica said. "His letter sounded so calm. He came here to tell the people about Jesus. They may have already known about God, but he probably told them that Jesus died for them so they could become God's children."

"Yes," James agreed. "I'm sure he was a godly man."

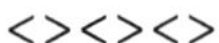

Greg came round to the cottage during the early part of the evening. James and Jessica were alone in the front room reading by one of the gas lanterns. James's parents were reading in the kitchen with the other lantern. When Greg heard they'd been to the police he looked scared, but calmed down when they told him it was about the water.

"Anyway, what's there to worry about?" James asked. "I'm sure Brian won't make trouble for you. You *are* friends, aren't you?"

Greg shrugged his broad shoulders. "You tell me. He seems so different."

"What do you mean?" James asked.

"Like ... well, you heard what he said in the hospital. Why weren't he glad I prayed for him?"

"He certainly didn't seem pleased," James

agreed. "But I wouldn't have expected you to pray."

"Why not?" Greg asked.

"I'm not sure really. It's just that you said the other day...."

"What about Brian then?" Greg asked. "Out on the hill he made all sorts of promises to God, but now he's better he don't care no more." He sounded quite upset at this. Almost indignant.

"People promise all sorts of things when they're in trouble," James said. "You should know that!"

"There's something in it, I think," Greg said. "Only you've got to try really hard."

"In what?" James asked after a pause.

"Well, you know." Greg looked embarrassed. He walked over to the window and looked out into the darkness. "You know. To do the sort of stuff what Holy Dan preaches about."

There was a long silence. Greg started wiping the window with his sleeve.

At last James said, "You can never become a real Christian by trying, if that's what you're thinking. It's just not possible. Mr. Peterson could explain it better, but that's the whole reason God sent his Son Jesus to this earth."

"Something to do with him dying, weren't it?" Greg asked. "I never could see the point of that."

"You've done wrong things that hurt God, and so have I," James explained.

"Who told you what I done?" Greg demanded,

starting to sound angry.

Jesus, help me say the right thing. "It's not just you, Greg," James said. "The Bible says there isn't anybody in the whole world who can come to God claiming they're already good enough. God loves you and he loves me. Instead of punishing *us,* he said his Son's death would count instead. You've got to do something about it though. It's ... a bit ... a bit like the bus we got from the hospital. We had to get *on* the bus or we wouldn't have got back. It's no good sitting in the bus shelter and hoping for the best."

"Then if I ask him to, he'll forgive me?" Greg asked, sounding surprised.

James hesitated a moment before answering, and Greg noticed it.

"You don't sound sure," he said.

"Oh, I'm sure all right," James said with a smile. "It's just that I don't want to give you the wrong idea."

"I thought there'd be a catch in it," Greg muttered, returning to the window.

"There's no catch," James said quickly, "but you saw what happened to Brian. He only wanted to be safe while he thought he was seriously hurt. He didn't want changes in his life."

"Supposing I *can't* change my life?" Greg asked. "I've tried before, but it didn't work. That's why I left off going to church."

James wished he'd spent a bit more time praying for Greg. He fetched his Bible from the windowsill. It was only lately he'd found just how much the Bible really meant to him. "There won't be any sermons," he assured Greg when he saw him eyeing the Bible anxiously.

James turned to the last book in the Bible. Revelation. After a bit of hunting he found verse twenty of chapter three. "There you are," he said, showing it to Greg. "It's Jesus speaking."

Greg read it out aloud. "'Behold, I stand at the door and knock. If anyone hears my voice and opens the door, I will come in to him and eat with him, and he with me.'"

After a suitable pause, James said, "It's like a house. We asked you into this cottage. You can ask Jesus into your house ... your life ... you know what it means. It says here that he's knocking. Now it's up to you whether you let him in or not. I've let him in and so has Jessica."

Greg nodded. "This cottage were nice and tidy when you asked me in. Mine ain't." He pointed to himself. "I mean me – my life."

"That doesn't matter." James made another silent prayer that Greg would understand. "Just ask him in and tell him to take charge of your life."

"Does this mean I won't get into no trouble?"

"God will forgive you," James said, "but that doesn't mean everyone else will. He's punished

Jesus for everything we've ever done wrong. Jesus has risen from the dead, so now you can ask him to let that punishment count for you, too."

Greg stayed silent as he read and re-read that verse. "Yes, I'd like to ask him. Maybe sometime soon."

"You'll not be sorry," James said quietly. "I know it's a real promise in the Bible. But don't do it soon – do it *now*."

Greg nodded. "Yes, all right, if you think I'm good enough to do it now."

James shook his head and smiled. "Don't you understand, Greg? No one's good enough. We *all* need God to wash us clean."

"What about Saint Cerig?" Greg asked. "Did he need to be washed?"

Jessica, who had been praying silently, had a sudden picture of Saint Cerig sitting in his well, furiously trying to scrub himself clean. But she stayed quiet, and continued praying.

"*Everyone* needs to be washed. You have to come exactly as you are – and you can come to God now." James said. "*I* can't do it for you."

And there, in the front room of the cottage, Greg knelt and asked God to forgive him. Then he asked Jesus to come into his life.

James looked at Jessica and smiled. They were children of God – all three of them!

Chapter Eleven

THE OLD VAN

The next day was Sunday. Greg was at church for the morning service. He sat with Jessica and James, much to the obvious surprise of some of the congregation. Two women muttered to each other in obvious disapproval, but most people gave Greg a welcoming smile, and a few even came across before the service started to say how good it was to see him. Jessica remembered back to the previous Sunday when Greg had threatened them and told them to stay away from the church. She decided to keep that memory to herself!

That afternoon Greg walked up the hill with them, and came back to tea at the cottage. James lent him his new Bible to take away, as long as he brought it back before the end of the holiday. He had the Bible on his phone, and if he wanted a printed copy he could always borrow Jessica's.

Then at the evening service Greg discovered he could buy one for himself from Mr. Peterson at the back of church, so James got his copy back sooner than expected.

<><><>

On Monday morning Jessica woke early and decided James shouldn't be allowed to go on sleeping. She crept down the stairs and to her surprise James was already dressed, with his two photographs on the kitchen table.

James had become used to sleeping on the sofa, which was just as well, for there was no hope of his bedroom ceiling being repaired while they were still there. All the owner of the cottage had done was to throw an old tarpaulin over that part of the roof, and weigh down each side with bricks. He'd said he'd get something done about it before the next people came.

James looked up at Jessica. "I was just having a good look at my two prints. I can hardly believe it, they're so sharp!"

"I'm glad," Jessica said, and she meant it. "I'm not so sure about the one of me, but I love the one you took from the tree when you were getting the kite."

James leaned over it again. "I'd no idea the tree was so high. You can see ever so far. Right over to Glastonbury. And you can even see into the old quarry."

Jessica took the print from him. "There's a van with a trailer or something in the quarry. It's parked by the old mineshaft."

James, who'd been examining his prints for quality rather than content, snatched it back. "You're right," he agreed. "There's a man with his back to us. He's wearing a hood, but he looks like he's tipping something into the shaft from a large container. Get the magnifying glass."

Jessica said her eyes were far too sleepy to see such fine detail, but she did as she was told. James's combined compass and magnifying glass was in his jacket pocket.

James took the glass and focused it on the photograph. "You're right, he *is* tipping something down the mineshaft! Here, you have a look."

Jessica did as she was told and gave a long sigh. Then she suddenly woke up. "Look at that! I'm sure that person is up to no good. We'll get your dad to take us to the police station again, with this evidence."

<><><>

The police station was at the far end of town. A bicycle was leaning up against the railings, but it looked too smart to be a police bike. Anyway, James wondered, did the police still use bicycles? There was no sign of a police car. The building was very old. The heavy door had a large brass doorknob.

Today there was a different policeman behind the desk, and James asked for the man who'd been on duty on Saturday.

"He's at home. We have a change of duties on Monday. Right, what can I do for you?"

Jessica spoke loudly across the high counter. "It's about the poisoned animals at Sheppingford."

"Come to confess, have you?" the policeman

asked wearily, then he suddenly looked interested. "No, I'm sorry. I was only pulling your legs. You came here on Saturday. I saw the report this morning. I'll get Detective Sergeant Dawes down to have a word with you. He's in charge of the case now. It seems as though you've stirred up some interest with your report."

James held up his photograph. "Just wait until he sees this!"

The Detective Sergeant was certainly interested, and he asked if he could make a copy of the print on the station scanner. The van had no name to identify it, he explained, and unfortunately the licence plate wasn't visible. But they might be able to trace it through a dark patch on the passenger door.

"I think the man is definitely emptying something, either onto the ground or into the mineshaft. The problem is, the trailer's in the way, so we can't see exactly what's going on. It could be a farmer or a builder or even someone from a factory. Sheppingford isn't too far from the motorway, so any driver who wanted to find a place to dump some dangerous waste can save himself a long journey and a lot of money by not going to an official waste treatment plant. Factories often get other people to dispose of their waste. Once it's left their gates, they're not bothered about it any more, even though by law they're still responsible."

"They ought to be in prison!" Jessica said angrily. "To think that those animals died because someone tried to save money. Greg was right – he ought to be locked up!"

The Detective Sergeant was pleasant, and the Two Jays were glad they'd been able to see him. "You leave any locking up to us, miss," he said with a smile. "On the other hand, if you see that van and trailer around the area, get in touch with us immediately. We'd like to catch him actually near the mineshaft, if possible, but hopefully before he gets the chance to empty something dangerous down there!"

"We'll keep a lookout," Jessica promised, "and I hope you get there in time to stop him. I can't help thinking of the animals."

<><><>

They saw Greg in the village on the way back. He looked happier, but became serious when he told them how he'd tried to see Brian Tucker that morning at the hospital. Brian had refused to see him.

"I went there specially on the bus. I only wanted to tell him what had happened to me, asking Jesus in," Greg explained, sounding hurt. "I didn't even get a chance to speak to him. He told me to clear off!"

"Perhaps you'll be able to tell him soon," James said. "Keep on praying for him."

Greg flicked his hair from his eyes. “There’s a funny thing about that. When I prayed for Brian on the hill, I did it to get out of trouble. Now, I prays just to talk to Jesus.” He turned away and kicked at a stone. “Oh, I know it sounds silly,” he muttered. “I ain’t very good at it, neither. I forget to say all those fancy bits like they sometimes says in church. All I say is, ‘This is Greg Hawker speaking,’ and then I just starts talking.”

James smiled. “I think it’s best not to put in the fancy bits. I don’t think you need them – not in private prayers.”

“I’m glad about that,” Greg said, with a sigh of relief. “I can’t remember how they goes anyhow! Mind you,” he said suddenly, “I’m still in trouble.”

“Oh?” James raised his eyebrows.

“My dad,” Greg explained. “He’s got together with Brian’s ma, and they’ve fair got it in for me!”

“But it was an accident – wasn’t it?”

Greg looked up quickly at James, and then stared at the ground. “Yes,” he said, “it were like I said. An accident.”

Jessica had been quiet up to now. “Have you told Mr. Peterson about you becoming a Christian?”

Greg shook his head again. “He wouldn’t understand. He probably thinks *everyone’s* a Christian. I wouldn’t like no minister to think I hadn’t been a proper Christian before.”

“Perhaps he’s been praying for you,” James

suggested. "After all, it did all seem a bit sudden."

"Not really sudden," Greg said with an unexpected smile. "It may have seemed a bit sort of sudden to you, but it were something that were bothering me for a long time. That's why I kept on at Brian to leave Discoverers. It weren't no business of mine, but every time I thought about the place, it hurt. Hurt me bad, see. I knew there were something in this Christian stuff, and a couple of year ago I nearly decided to follow Jesus. Then I thought I didn't want no *changes* in my life."

Greg took a deep breath, apparently exhausted at the end of such a long speech. There was silence for a moment. Having got his breath back, he continued. "Perhaps you're right. I think I will go and see Mr. Peterson. He might be able to do something to help." Greg started to walk away. "Perhaps I'll go and see him now. I'm in trouble, see. Big trouble."

They said goodbye, but when Greg was a few yards away he turned and came back. "That accident. I don't know what to do about it. It weren't no accident, see. Not a *real* accident."

James gasped. "You didn't hurt Brian on purpose?"

"No," Greg said, "not on purpose. But I sort of lost my temper with him, and thought I'd teach him a lesson. Just to frighten him, see."

James looked at Greg. "But you told us it was an

accident, and you let us believe you."

Greg nodded and looked miserable.

"So you were just laughing at us being taken in like that," James went on.

"No, I never!" Greg said firmly. "I wanted someone to be on my side, see. That's why I let you believe me. Anyway, I didn't mean for him to fall. I shot at him just to scare him. And then he let go of the branch. So I suppose it were my fault."

"But you can trust us," Jessica said, "so why couldn't you tell us the truth before?"

"Scared I were. Once I'd said it were an accident, I had to stick to it. I'll tell you one thing. If I hadn't become a Christian, I'd never be letting on." Greg sounded depressed. "In some ways I wish I hadn't become one. A great help it seems to have been to me!"

"You won't find all your troubles are solved," James told him. "I'll tell you what. When you go to see Mr. Peterson, tell him the truth about the accident. He might be able to help you sort everything out."

Greg looked more cheerful. "Yes, he'd know what to do, wouldn't he."

James nodded. "And God would know as well. Don't forget he's your Father now."

Greg looked worried. "*Father*?" Then he smiled and nodded. "Yes, I get it now. A very *good* Father. You know what?" He pointed at James. "I think I'm *glad* I handed my life over to Jesus. Well ... I hopes I am."

James and Jessica arranged to meet Greg at the well after lunch. They were planning to inspect the rows of stones they'd already uncovered from under the leaves and the mud to see if they could make any sense of them. It seemed a shame that there were so few stones. Certainly not nearly enough to build a dwelling or chapel, or whatever could have been there originally. The purpose of the round holes in some of the stones puzzled them.

Greg turned up about three o'clock, wearing his oldest clothes. He said it would be such a messy job cleaning up the old stones, that he didn't want to risk getting into any more trouble at home.

"Is this where you think the heads belong?" Greg asked, pointing to the two holes cut into the rock face.

"That's what we think," James said. "Anyway, it would be great if they did."

Greg was thoughtful. "Why don't we try them? I'll go and fetch them."

"You can't!" James was shocked. Surely Greg wouldn't try to pull them out of the church pulpit.

Greg laughed at his concern. "No, it were only a joke. I could model them for you though."

"How?" James sounded interested.

"In modelling clay. I does a lot of modelling and stuff, and I bakes it hard in the oven. If I goes and starts it now, I should be able to get both them heads finished by tea. Come with me to the church if you like. You might be able to see something about them. You seem to be able to think of some clever things."

Coming from someone older than him and Jessica, James felt pleased with the compliment. It seemed strange that they were now on such friendly terms with Greg. Their first meeting had seemed extremely unpromising!

Greg said he would go off first and collect some modelling clay from his home. They would all meet in the church. As James watched Greg walk off down the lane he smiled to himself. On the one occasion that Greg had changed into really old clothes, he weren't going to do any messy clearing!

James wanted to check out the old quarry again, to see if he could work out why the dye had gone to one well and not the other. There was no need to keep away from the quarry now that the dye had done its work.

As they reached the entrance to the quarry, James turned to Jessica, but she was looking in the other direction.

"Quick," she said, dragging James to one side. "Hide behind these bushes."

Along the track, driving slowly and quietly, he could see an old white van and trailer. *And the van had a dark patch on the passenger door!*

Chapter Twelve

THE FIRST SOLUTION

In horror the Two Jays watched the driver turn the van into the entrance.

James felt helpless. "What shall we do?"

Jessica already had her phone in her hand. "I'm phoning for the police. And we don't go into the quarry and interfere. We stay here."

James thought Jessica sounded completely in control of what could be a dangerous situation. "Definitely stay here," he whispered.

As Jessica finished the call to the police, a slight noise from further down the track made James jump. Now who was coming? Someone on an old bicycle. Not the police. It was Mr. Slade who worked in the quarry. Was he mixed up in all this poisoning? Perhaps he was getting a share of the money the owner of the van saved by not using an official waste disposal site.

Now a car was coming. It was being driven fast. What a relief – the police!

Jessica jumped out from behind the thick bushes where they were hiding by the entrance and waved the car down.

"The van's still there," James told the two police officers in the car. "Mr. Slade has gone in there on his bike. You were very quick."

"A bit of luck, really," the police officer explained as he swung the car across the quarry entrance. "Is this the only way out? Good. We were close by when we got the message over the radio. Our headquarters put out a call for all cars to guard the roads in the area. This is a serious business. Next time it might not be only animals that get poisoned. Ah, there's the van. Caught in the act, as they say."

The driver of the van, the hood of his coat hiding his head, was holding a large polythene container. It was impossible to see if it was full or empty. Mr. Slade's bicycle lay on the ground and he was shouting at the driver.

"You've come just in time," he called to the police. "This man was going to tip these chemicals down the old mine."

Going to? James looked at Jessica. Then the police *had* arrived in time. But what did Mr. Slade mean? Did he have nothing to do with it? Was he only here by chance? It certainly looked that way.

The van driver protested his innocence. There must be some mistake. His load was perfectly harmless. He was quite sure he would be allowed to tip here.

The policeman pointed to the large polythene container which was covered with danger warnings. The van driver shook his head and insisted he'd never been near the place before. James took his phone out of his pocket and went to the photo gallery.

He found the photograph he'd taken from high up in the oak tree and pulled the quarry part of the picture larger, until the van could be seen clearly, with the large black mark on the passenger door. The policeman studied it, then handed the phone to the driver who was now looking extremely worried.

"Not been here before? Then how do you explain this?"

The van driver stared at it. "Yes, well, I suppose I might have been. No harm would have been done." He nodded towards Mr. Slade. "I'd have dumped the load and gone if this old man hadn't come poking his nose in."

The policeman spoke into his radio. He looked at the driver in disgust. "This old man, as you call him, is Mr. Slade. He happens to be working in this quarry."

James was glad Mr. Slade wasn't involved. Dumping chemicals was such a horrible thing to do. His father had been right about Mr. Slade being innocent. The police had arrived in time to prevent the water being poisoned again. Catching the van driver had been exciting enough. But when Greg had finished modelling the two heads, there might be even more exciting things to discover!

Chapter Thirteen

ANOTHER DISCOVERY

It was Tuesday. James and Jessica had just finished breakfast, and were getting ready to go to the old well. Greg was going to be there with the clay heads. There was a knock at the front door and James looked out of the window. There, leaning against the garden wall was Mr. Slade's old bike.

"I've come to thank you," Mr. Slade told the Two Jays.

"Thank us?" Jessica asked.

Mr. Slade smiled. "Is ... er ... is your father in?"

"Mr. Cooper is. He's not *my* father," Jessica explained. "He's James's father. He's my Uncle Clive. I'm Jessica Green."

Mr. Slade coughed. "Sorry, I thought you two was brother and sister. I'm afraid I may have seemed an unpleasant old man when I chased you both from the quarry when you first got here. Ah, good morning, Mr. Cooper."

James's father had heard voices, and come to investigate. "I'm glad you've called in," he said to Mr. Slade. "I'm sorry I came round to your house and more or less accused you of causing the trouble with the water."

Mr. Slade smiled. He seemed more at ease now. "*I've* come to apologize, really. I can see why you thought I'd done it. Once these two traced where the water come from, it made sense to blame me at the quarry." He scratched his head. "Worried I were. You see, I'd already made that discovery myself. I knew the water come through the quarry on its way to that well."

"You mean you knew that the man with the van was dumping poisonous chemicals?" James said.

"Bless you, no! But I thought *I'd* caused all the trouble. You see, whenever I had a lot of building rubble to clear away, I tipped it down the old mine. I expect you saw it was nearly full. Of course, it's not my quarry really. Then when them animals started dying I got worried. I thought it were something in my stuff that were doing it."

"You can't have had enough rubble to fill it almost to the top," Jessica said, slightly puzzled by the old man's story.

"People had been tipping there for a long time. Not household rubbish though. Garden rubbish and stuff like that. That's how I discovered the water ran to the well by the rock face down below. Every time I tipped soil there, the water in it would turn brown for a day or more."

There was a pause while Mr. Slade looked awkward. "I ... I want to say ... say sorry again for shouting at these two."

"We didn't mind," James said. "We guessed we weren't wanted!"

"No, no, it were all my fault. I really thought the poison were coming from my stuff. That made me afraid someone would find out."

"But it wasn't anything to do with you," Jessica interrupted, a frown on her face.

"Ah, but I didn't know that at the time. Besides, the poison *were* coming from the old mineshaft! If I'd spoken up, the trouble might have been sorted out quicker. Instead, I tried to keep everyone away."

Mr. Cooper assured Mr. Slade that they understood how he had felt.

"Anyway," Mr. Slade continued, "I'd like to say thank you to one and all for what you done. I'd never seen that van driver before in my life. Said he thought it would be safe at that time of the afternoon, and he thought the liquids would stay in the mine. Daft! An agricultural contractor from ten mile away. Had a surplus of brushwood killer and a lot of other chemicals left over from different jobs, and were too mean to dispose of it legally. Pah! He admitted he's been coming here for some time. Most of his loads were completely safe — but not *every* one!"

"Do you know what's going to happen to the mineshaft now?" Mr. Cooper asked.

"Well," Mr. Slade said slowly, "I've heard tell

them's going to cap the old shaft and seal it good and proper. The Environment Agency and other officials will be tracing the water supply. After all, the water in that well of yours has to be going somewhere next. Probably it gets much too diluted to do more harm once it leaves the well, but..." He seemed to have run out of breath, or out of ideas. Then he turned to Mr. Cooper. "Anywise, them two here did a good and proper job, them did."

James and Jessica said they were glad to have helped, and Mr. Slade was given a large mug of tea. Eventually the Two Jays were ready to leave. Jessica said she was wearing wellington boots again, because the ground by the well was getting very muddy from everyone walking around there. Mr. Slade said he'd push his bike along with them. He'd heard about their discovery at the well from Mr. Peterson, and wanted to see it for himself.

As they walked together, Mr. Slade said he was quite sure they couldn't have possibly found anything to do with Saint Cerig. *Everyone* knew where Saint Cerig's well was. Hadn't his father and grandfather told him it was in the field? They'd told him, when he was a child. Yes, *everyone* had been told that! All the same, he'd like to see the pattern on the wall – just for interest.

There was no sign of Greg when they reached the well. Perhaps he'd been grounded, or even run away again. Nor was there any sign of the two heads.

"That's not a chapel!" Mr. Slade exclaimed when he saw the stones now laid out on the ground. "I know what you've found. You've found the remains of the old shepherd's hut."

James said nothing. It couldn't be true. Not after all the work they'd done. For one thing, a shepherd wouldn't have carved figures on the rock face. Would he? And then there were the heads. Greg had a letter – or a copy of a letter – from Saint Cerig mentioning the heads. There, right in front of them were the two holes cut in the rock specially for them to fit in. Not a shepherd's hut. *Couldn't* be!

"I remember it when it were standing," Mr. Slade continued, for James and Jessica were too stunned to argue. "There were a big elm tree up there, and one night it fell on the old hut and knocked him flat."

"Was it still being used?" Jessica asked quietly, thinking there might have been sheep inside at the time.

"No, no. It had no roof. Never had, as far as I can remember. Mind you, I'm not saying it *were* a shepherd's hut, but that's what we used to call it."

"What happened to all the stones?" James asked, because there certainly weren't enough left for any sort of building.

Mr. Slade picked up a stick and leaned against

it. "Ah, I remember now. That was a cold, hard winter. You don't get winters like that now, that you don't. First we cut up the old tree and sold it round the houses for firewood. Kept many a poor family warm that winter, did that old elm."

James wondered how much the villagers had paid for the firewood, and whether they were poor before or after they'd bought it! "What about the stones?" he asked, feeling that Mr. Slade might be the only person in Sheppingford to know the answer. "Did they get taken away too?"

"Stones?" Mr. Slade asked. "Stones? Let me see. Yes. Now, something happened to——. Why, that's they down there." He pointed to the cleaned stones that the Two Jays and Greg had placed nearby.

"But they can't all be there," James said. "There aren't nearly enough."

"You're quite right, young fellow. Yes, now I comes to think about it, we did do something with them stones. I'm blessed if I can remember what at this moment."

James could see that Jessica was hopping about impatiently, and he felt like joining her.

"Ah, now wait a moment." Mr. Slade raised a finger. "Them's not far away. Farmer Osborne wanted them to finish off a job on his pigsty. My pa was doing the building work for him. We needed them for the front. Well-cut stones they was. Hardly the thing for pigs, but——"

"Can you take us to see?" James asked eagerly. "We're sure they're part of Saint Cerig's chapel. We think it was built right here."

"Bless me, you could be right after all."

James noticed the excitement in Mr. Slade's voice as the old man went over to the stones. "You're right. No shepherd would have bothered to do all this. These stones was cut to fit together and stay that way. See? No, of course it wouldn't mean much to you. Me, it's my job. If we can get the rest of them stones, I think I could put some of the lower ones back as they was."

"In the right order?" Jessica sounded amazed.

"I'll do my best, miss. These stones have been well cut. They may all look the same to you, but each of these large stones has been made to fit against the next." Mr. Slade examined the stones again. "Of course," he continued, "I should have noticed how well the stones we took for the pigsty were cut when I came here with my pa fifty year ago. I were only learning the craft then, and I were more interested in a bit of work than in — than in all this history. 'Live each day as it comes', I've always thought, 'and let the past look after itself.'"

"Are there enough stones in the pigsty to go the whole way up to the roof?" James asked.

Mr. Slade shook his head and looked thoughtful.

James was afraid Mr. Slade was losing interest,

but he needn't have worried.

"Just two courses of stone here as far as I can remember. Then it was sheets of corrugated iron. Them's long gone. I guess the original building had timber for the top part, filled in with what we call wattle and daub."

He caught sight of James's frown. "Sticks, my lad, woven this way and that, and filled in with hard clay. It was used a lot in the old days. And see them sockets?" He pointed to the round holes in some of the stones that had puzzled James and Jessica. "Them would have held thick posts to support the roof. Come on, you two young 'uns, let's get down to see Farmer Osborne. It's time them pigs of his had a new sty!"

Mr. Osborne was quite caught up by the enthusiasm of his three visitors. He laughed at the idea of his pigsty having anything to do with "that old saint," as he put it. Yes, he would let them take the stones away as soon as they wanted to take them. Mr. Slade — as a stonemason — said he could soon replace them with other stones, but Farmer Osborne said concrete building blocks would do perfectly well for pigs.

He explained that the sty wasn't being used at the moment, so there was no hurry. There was only one wall that would have to be replaced. He had some blocks round the back somewhere, so it only needed Mr. Slade to help lay them.

As far as James could see, the stones in the sty were identical with the ones at the well.

"I'll get my tractor and trailer, and we'll take them round to the well straight away," Farmer Osborne said. "To tell you the truth, I'm starting to feel a bit guilty about it. I were only a nipper fifty year ago — it were in my father's time. All the same, I don't like to think of them stones being stuck here with only pigs for company!"

The stones, which were cut straight, only had a loose mortar to bind them together. If they'd been cemented, they would have been stuck together for good.

The wall came to bits easily, and the stones were fairly clean, except those at ground level. Jessica moved well away and held her nose while the farmer hosed them down with a powerful jet of water.

Greg was waiting when they returned to the well. "I'm sorry I couldn't come back yesterday," he explained. "There were a bit of trouble with my dad. I heard about what you done with catching that van driver. I'm glad he were caught. I just hope no one else comes tipping anything."

James, forgetting that Greg had promised to model the heads from the church, was glad of the extra help. The stones were heavy to unload.

The foundation stones deep in the ground had now been cleared by Greg and the Two Jays. Mr.

Slade fitted first one, and then another of the large stones on top.

"I suppose it's all right to be doing this," Jessica said, her voice showing some doubt. "You know what I mean. Is it all right to muck about with an old building like this?"

James laughed. "It's been pretty mucked about with already!" Then he became serious. "Yes, I know what you mean."

Mr. Slade's experience came to their rescue. "I can't see no harm being done, and it will only be two more rows. I'm not going to use cement. It will be what we calls a dry wall. If anyone wants to do the job properly later, they can use a soft mortar."

"You're right," James agreed. "We'll be doing them a favour. Even if we only rebuild a bit, all the stones will be here. We ought to let someone know what we've done. It would be a shame if the stones got taken away again."

"Don't you worry about that," Mr. Slade said, with laughter in his eyes. "Everyone in the village will know about this before the day be out. Farmer Osborne isn't going to keep quiet about the discovery in his pigsty!"

"Then let's hurry up," Jessica urged. "We'll try and get the two rows finished before we get any visitors."

Mr. Slade pulled a pocket watch from his old waistcoat. "Time for my lunch. I'll be back afterwards," he promised.

Jessica, impatient as ever, asked if they could make a start by themselves. Mr. Slade warned them not to try. The stones were far too heavy for them to lift on their own. In any case, didn't they want their lunch? They did, and the party split up, agreeing to meet again at two.

Chapter Fourteen

THE SECOND SOLUTION

Mr. Slade reappeared on time. He had three thick wooden poles strapped to his bicycle. He explained that the stones were too heavy for him to lift into place alone, and he didn't want the others dropping them on their toes. With the three poles and a pulley, he assured them he would be able to manage it easily, if they helped a bit. Greg came soon after, wearing old leather gloves to help with the lifting.

James thought that an hour would be plenty of time to lay two rows of stones. But Mr. Slade seemed to take so long with each stone. There were no short cuts if it was going to be done properly, he kept telling them. James thought it might be a bit quicker if Mr. Slade didn't take so long moving each stone this way and that, in order to get the correct spacing of the post sockets in some of the stones. It was taking along time, but he had to admit that Mr. Slade was making a very good job of it.

Jessica was having a bit of a rest. Sitting under the trees near the spot where a few of the stones had been lying, she began poking in the soft earth. Her stick dug up a couple of small stones, but no more ancient glass or china. Then she saw the neck of a brown earthenware bottle. She poked a bit harder and revealed more of the bottle. It seemed to be unbroken. There was some writing under the mud that covered it.

James, Greg and Mr. Slade heard her squeal, and stopped work to see what she'd found. Jessica washed it in the well, knowing the water was now safe.

"A ginger beer bottle," Mr. Slade said. "'Tis only a bit of rubbish."

Jessica read the inscription on the side. BOTTLED IN GLASTONBURY. "It's not rubbish," she protested. "It may have been rubbish once, but I think it's great. I'm going to clean it properly back at the cottage. We found some broken things here last Friday." She hesitated a moment. What seemed rubbish to Mr. Slade was marvellous to her. Might this bottle be valuable? If so, she would be stealing it from whoever owned the land. "I don't know if I ought to keep it," she said. "Whose land is this?"

"'Tis Farmer Osborne's," Mr. Slade said. "He won't mind. I should just take it along home with you."

Jessica put the bottle safely under the holly tree. "I'm sure he wouldn't mind. All the same, I'm going to ask him. When I get home I'm going to put this on display for everyone to see, but I wouldn't feel happy about it if I didn't ask."

Greg nodded in agreement, and James could understand exactly how she felt. It would be much better to ask.

The stones in the second row were difficult to put on. It needed the four of them to assist with the lifting, helped by the three poles and the pulley. Mr. Slade seemed quite exhausted by the end, and it was nearly dusk.

James looked at the low walls. It was now possible to see the exact size of the place, and it was really, really small. He didn't fancy the idea of living there himself.

"This were never no shepherd's hut, nor were it a chapel," Mr. Slade said, with a puzzled frown on his face. "Not a proper chapel. More like a shelter for the saint. That's what it were. Just enough room for the man to live in. I think it would have become known as a chapel because he prayed in here and studied the Bible perhaps."

"A hermitage," Jessica said.

James suddenly felt happy. As the walls had been taking shape on the ground, he'd been having horrible doubts whether this could be a chapel. A hermitage. He liked the thought of that. Hermitage was a nice name. He could picture Saint Cerig sheltering in here day after day. Not much room for him, but enough to keep the weather off. "We ought to get a plaque up. 'Saint Cerig's Hermitage.'" He smiled at Jessica. "Isn't it good! A real hermitage. We were right about this being the proper Saint Cerig's well just outside the door."

Jessica shared James's feelings. To be a chapel, other people would have had to come and sing hymns and things, or whatever they did back then. There was only just enough room for the four of them to stand inside, and they weren't even singing! There would have been a church in the village. Maybe even the one there now. That must have been the house of God that Saint Cerig was talking about in his letter.

"How did Saint Cerig manage to cut the stones so well?" James asked, running his hands over the low walls.

"I don't suppose he did it himself," Mr. Slade explained. "I could do it with hand tools, but then it's my job. I expect there was a local stonemason who did it for him. Perhaps they stones come from my quarry. It might have been one of my great-great-grandparents who cut them."

"More like great-great-great-great-great——" Jessica added, but she was interrupted by James.

"Did you make the heads with modelling clay, Greg?"

"They're at home. I, er ... they're not very.... My dad smashed them up, see. But I have plenty more clay."

"Come on," Jessica said kindly, "let's go and make some more. I'm sure Mr. Peterson will let us turn the church lights on if we explain what we want to do."

Mr. Peterson showed great interest, and promised to have a look at their building first thing in the morning. The Two Jays, however, had every intention of letting Greg make the heads immediately, and returning that evening to the site with the lanterns from the cottage. James's parents had given them permission to be out late, as long as Greg was with them. A few days ago it would have been permission to stay out late as long as Greg *wasn't* with them!

They finally got back to the hermitage with the replica heads, although Greg had not been able to bake them hard in time.

The three stood the gas lantern at the foot of the rock face and looked again at the carvings. They stood out remarkably well, even after several hundred years. The place was so sheltered, and for many years it had apparently been used as a shepherd's hut.

Greg held the heads carefully. "I'm glad we've built the bottom part of the walls up again. Now let's try fitting them heads in the holes in the rock." He handed the heads to James. "Be carful how you holds 'em. Them's still a bit soft."

"I'll be careful. Now if I put one of them here ...

and the other one in this side ... it wouldn't be very interesting." James looked puzzled. "No, there must be more to it."

Jessica tried next. "They look so real," she said. "Look how Greg's copied all the lines on the faces. You can even see which way the eyes are looking!"

James reached forward. "Quick, I think I know! I never thought of the eyes. Which way are they looking?"

Jessica gave another squeal. "This one is looking down at the ground over there, and the other is looking at the ground ... on the other side." She frowned. "What the use of that?"

James came forward and changed the heads over. "Now they're both looking at the same place on the floor," he said, gasping in excitement. "Don't you see what that means?"

"I can guess," Greg said. "Where's the spade?"

Greg picked up the spade and knocked hard on the ground, there and all around, where they had earlier uncovered several large, flat stones. One of them sounded hollow.

"It's not *exactly* where the heads are looking," Jessica said doubtfully.

"I know," James said cheerfully. "These are only models. Greg's done them well, but the eyes may not be *exactly* right. We didn't think it was going to be important."

"Let's have that stone up," Greg suggested, his

voice hushed.

They fitted the spade in a crack and levered back. Slowly the large flat stone came up. As soon as he could, James pushed a thick stick into the gap, to stop the stone falling back. Again they levered, and with six grasping hands it came up.

Cold, musty air met their eager faces. James shone one of the lanterns into the hole.

He seemed to be looking into a low cave. There was black mud and deep puddles on the uneven floor. The walls were flat but rough, and not like the cave they'd been down at Cheddar. Perhaps someone had cut the sides away to make the place larger. He leaned in a bit further. If the others held his legs, he'd be able to touch the floor.

It was interesting, but it definitely didn't lead anywhere. He could see all four walls. It was even smaller than the hermitage. The place was empty apart from a pile of stones.

"It's ever so damp," he called out. His voice echoed, and bits of dirt fell into the largest puddle directly below. "No one could have slept down here."

Jessica and Greg knelt down with him.

"Perhaps it wasn't so wet in those days," Jessica suggested. She poked a long stick into the water. "There's just about enough room to get down. Pass me the lantern. No, it's all right, I'm not *going* to climb down. I'm just looking." Jessica leaned over further and shone the lantern to the corners. “There doesn’t seem to be anything down here, except a heap of stones at the end.”

“I wonder why the stones are there like that,” James said, his voice quiet. There was something about this place he couldn’t understand. “I could roll my jeans up and get down to have a look. You can hold onto my arms just in case there’s a deep part.”

“No,” Greg said, equally quietly. He’d been very silent up to now. “Don’t go in. You know who’s under them stones, don’t you?”

James stopped at once. “Do you mean it’s where——?” He said no more. How could he? In awed silence they all just looked.

James could understand now why he’d felt so strange when he’d first looked into the small underground room. This was where Saint Cerig had hidden when danger was near. It was also where the heads had given his secret away, and where his body had been hidden from everyone for the past seven hundred years or so.

After a few minutes they replaced the stone and stood in the lamplight, staring at the patterns on the rock face that they now believed was one of the inside walls of the hermitage.

“I still don’t see how the heads gave him away,” Jessica said with a shiver.

“I think I know,” James said softly. “He had the

cave underneath to hide in. Perhaps he even slept down there on a raised wooden bed to keep out of the water. Those old hermits seemed to have led harsh lives. I think he made the heads look at the entrance."

"Perhaps he was lonely," Jessica interrupted, "and the heads became like real people to him. He'd see them every time he came up."

Greg nodded. "And when the robbers – or whatever they was – come, they guessed Saint Cerig was hiding. Then they saw where the heads was looking and pulled that stone up. How very sad. I expect, as Jessica says, they was like friends to him. That's why he wanted them kept safe."

"Poor old Saint Cerig." Jessica turned away so the two boys couldn't see her eyes. "I wonder who buried him here. I expect it was the villagers. I can almost picture it all."

James found there was a lump in his throat, the saint seemed so real.

<><><>

The next morning a crowd of local people joined the Coopers and Jessica at the well. Then Greg arrived with Mr. and Mrs. Peterson. Congratulations were given to all concerned.

James felt like making a speech, thanking Mr. Slade and Farmer Osborne for their part. Somehow his idea fell to pieces when Mr. Peterson made a speech of his own, thanking the Two Jays and Greg for discovering the real well of Saint Cerig. Mr. Peterson seemed to have said everything there was to say, so James kept quiet.

James's mother thought more scrubbing would help the flagstones on the floor, and offered to give a hand in the afternoon. Right now she had to get back to get the lunch ready. Gradually everyone drifted away, leaving Greg, James and Jessica alone.

Greg had brought a brown paper package which he'd put to one side. He picked it up and looked at the ground, seeming embarrassed. "For you," he said quietly.

James wondered what it could be. Liquorice allsorts? Popcorn? Greg opened the bag for them.

"I er ... I er, thought you might like them, see. A sort of souvenir of your holiday. One for each of you."

"They're fantastic," James said, taking hold of a beautifully detailed clay model of one of the heads. Jessica took the other. The clay had been baked hard.

Jessica felt the excitement of the whole holiday run through her. If souvenirs were to help you remember a place and a good time, then this was the best sort of souvenir anyone could have — and the best sort of holiday. Then she remembered she'd not yet bought a present for her parents. Anyway, they had a few days left in Sheppingford.

She counted on her fingers. It was Wednesday evening now. They might dig up some more old bottles. She could use them as presents. Farmer Osborne had said she could keep anything she found. If she wanted to dig for more, that was all right by him. He thanked her for asking for permission, but said he had no use at all for old things like that. "If they was any good, they wouldn't have been throwed away!"

Jessica was only too glad to get the go-ahead, and planned to see just how many more things she could find between now and Saturday morning when they would have to go home.

"I'm glad you likes them," Greg said. "I'd often wondered why them two heads was in the church. They always seemed to be trying to say something. There were a write-up about them in the paper a couple of weeks ago. It said that——"

"—— they would have a tale to tell if they could talk!" Jessica put in, remembering what Mr. Peterson had said.

Greg laughed. "Something like that. Not that they said anything. Not with their mouths, anyway. They told a lot with their eyes!"

"They're fantastic," James told him. "They're too good to give to us. Oughtn't they stay here in the old chapel ... no, sorry, hermitage? After all, it might be rebuilt properly one day. Mr. Peterson has told the museum about it."

"No," Greg said firmly. "I've made two more for here, see. I might ... well, I might make some for Mr. Peterson as well. Oh, I meant to say – Brian comes out of hospital tomorrow. I think there's going to be trouble when he does. Mr. Peterson says he'll help me if ... well, you know.... Anyway, I've not heard from the police yet, but I know I'm going to. And it's bad with my dad. He don't like I being a Christian and going to church."

James looked at Greg and felt so helpless. Here was someone older than he was, and very different in so many ways. And yet they were able to share the same heavenly Father who cared for each of his children.

"You'll have to show him what knowing Jesus means to your life now," Jessica said. "Let him see the new Greg."

Greg nodded. "You've got something there. Yes, the new Greg, with a new heavenly Father. A *good* Father."

James had come to like Greg. He would always treasure the carefully modelled head Greg had made for him. Mr. Peterson would be sure to help Greg if the police took things further. There was nothing he could think of to say that would help, except, "We'll be praying for you, Greg. And thanks for the model heads."

Greg looked surprised. "Don't thank me. I come here to thank you, but I didn't know how to do it.

That's why I made them." He looked surprisingly pleased with everything. The thought of the possible trouble that lay ahead didn't show. "Anyway, you've helped me a lot. Everything seems ... seems so good now."

"I'm glad," James said. "Mr. Peterson will be able to answer a lot more of your questions on being a Christian than we've been able to do." Greg or Mr. Peterson might also be able to help Brian find Jesus. He and Jessica were already praying together for Brian.

The Two Jays turned to go. It had been a great holiday adventure. Two mysteries – the poisoned water and the two heads – and both of them solved. James was glad Jessica had been able to come with him to Sheppingford. Somehow they always managed to do something exciting when they were together.

"See you after lunch," James called over his shoulder to Greg.

Greg nodded and gave a cheerful smile. "Okay. And in case I can't get away – thanks!"

THE END

"Behold, I stand at the door and knock. If anyone hears my voice and opens the door, I will come in to him and eat with him, and he with me" (Revelation 3:20).

They who wait for the LORD
shall renew their strength;
They shall mount up
with wings like eagles;
They shall run and not be weary;
They shall walk and not faint.
(Isaiah 40:31)

About White Tree Publishing

White Tree Publishing publishes mainstream evangelical Christian literature in paperback and eBook formats, for people of all ages, by many different authors. We aim to make our eBooks available free for all eBook devices, but some distributors will only list our eBooks free at their discretion, and may make a small charge for some titles – but they are still great value!

We rely on our readers to tell their families, friends and churches about our books. Social media is a great way of doing this. Please pass the word on to Christian TV and radio networks. Also, write a positive review on the seller's/distributor's website if you are able.

The full list of our published and forthcoming Christian books in both paperbacks and eBooks is on our website www.whitetreepublishing.com. Please visit there regularly for updates.

Chris Wright has three grownup children, and lives in the West Country of England where he is a home group leader with his local church. More books by Chris Wright for young readers are on the next pages. His personal website is:
www.rocky-island.com

The Dark Tunnel Adventure
The Second Jays Story
Chris Wright

James and Jessica, the Two Jays, are on holiday in the Derbyshire Peak District, staying near Dakedale Manor, which has been completely destroyed in a fire. Did young Sam Stirling burn his family home down? Miss Parkin, the housekeeper, says he did, and she can prove it. Sam says he didn't, but can't prove it. But Sam has gone missing. James and Jessica believe the truth lies behind one of the old iron doors inside the disused railway tunnel.

eBook ISBN: 978-0-9957594-0-4

Paperback ISBN: 978-1-5206386-3-8
5x8 inches
Available from major internet stores
$5.99 £4.95

The Cliff Edge Adventure
The Third Two Jays Story
Chris Wright

James and Jessica's Aunt Judy lives in a lonely guest house perched on top of a crumbling cliff on the west coast of Wales. She is moving out with her dog for her own safety, because she has been warned that the waves from the next big storm could bring down a large part of the cliff – and her house with it. Cousins James and Jessica, the Two Jays, are helping her sort through her possessions, and they find an old papyrus page they think could be from an ancient copy of one of the Gospels. Two people are extremely interested in having it, but can either of them be trusted? James and Jessica are alone in the house. It's dark, the electricity is off, and the worst storm in living memory is already battering the coast. *Is there someone downstairs?*

eBook ISBN: 978-0-9957594-4-2

Paperback ISBN: 9781-5-211370-3-1
$5.99 £4.95

The Midnight Farm Adventure
The Fourth Two Jays Story
Chris Wright

What is hidden in the old spoil tip by the disused Midnight Mine? Two men have permission to dig there, but they don't want anyone watching -- especially not Jessica and James, the Two Jays. And where is Granfer Joe's old tin box, full of what he called his treasure? The Easter holiday at Midnight Farm in Cornwall isn't as peaceful as

James's parents planned. An early morning bike ride nearly ends in disaster, and with the so-called Hound of the Baskervilles running loose, things turn out to be decidedly dangerous. This is the fourth Two Jays adventure story. You can read them in any order, although each one goes forward slightly in time.

eBook ISBN: 978-1-9997899-1-6

Paperback ISBN: 978-1-5497148-3-2
200 pages 5x8 inches
$5.99 £4.95

The Merlin Adventure
Chris Wright

When Daniel, Emma, Charlie and Julia, the Four Merlins, set out to sail their model boat on the old canal, strange and dangerous things start to happen. Then Daniel and Julia make a discovery they want to share with the others.

eBook ISBN: 978-0-9954549-2-7

Paperback ISBN: 9785-203447-7-5

5x8 inches 180 pages
Available from major internet stores

The Hijack Adventure
Chris Wright

Anna's mother has opened a transport café, but why do the truck drivers avoid stopping there? An accident in the road outside brings Anna a new friend, Matthew. When they get trapped in a broken down truck with Matthew's dog, Chip, their adventure begins.

eBook ISBN: 978-0-9954549-6-5

Paperback ISBN: 978-1-5203448-0-5
5x8 inches 140 pages
Available from major internet stores

The Seventeen Steps Adventure
Chris Wright

When Ryan's American cousin, Natalie, comes to stay with him in England, a film from their Gran's old camera holds some surprise photographs, and they discover there's more to photography than taking selfies! But where are the Seventeen Steps, and has a robbery been planned to take place there?

eBook ISBN: 978-0-9954549-7-2

Paperback ISBN: 978-1-5203448-6-7
5x8 inches 132 pages

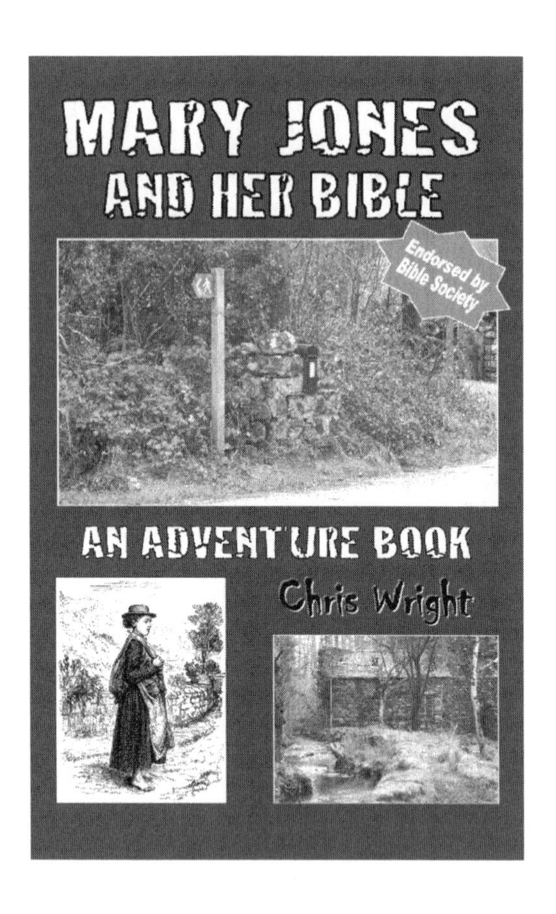

Mary Jones and Her Bible
An Adventure Book
Chris Wright
The true story of Mary Jones's and her Bible
with a clear Christian message and optional puzzles
(Some are easy, some tricky, and some amusing)

Mary Jones saved for six years to buy a Bible of her own. In 1800, when she was 15, she thought she had saved enough, so she walked barefoot for 26 miles (more than 40km) over a mountain pass and through deep valleys in Wales to get one. That's when she discovered there were none for sale!

You can travel with Mary Jones today in this book by following clues, or just reading the story. Either way, you will get to Bala where Mary went, and if you're really quick you may be able to discover a Bible just like Mary's in the market!

The true story of Mary Jones has captured the imagination for more than 200 years. For this book, Chris Wright has looked into the old records and discovered even more of the story, which is now in this unforgettable account of Mary Jones and her Bible. Solving puzzles is part of the fun, but the whole story is in here to read and enjoy whether you try the puzzles or not. Just turn the page, and the adventure continues. It's time to get on the trail of Mary Jones!

eBook ISBN: ISBN: 978-0-9933941-5-7

Paperback ISBN 978-0-9525956-2-5
5.5 x 8.5 inches
156 pages of story, photographs, line drawings and puzzles

Pilgrim's Progress
An Adventure Book
Chris Wright

Travel with young Christian as he sets out on a difficult and perilous journey to find the King. Solve the puzzles and riddles along the way, and help Christian reach the Celestial City. Then travel with his friend Christiana. She has four young brothers who can sometimes be a bit of a problem.

Be warned, you will meet giants and lions – and even dragons! There are people who don't want Christian and Christiana to reach the city of the King and his Son. But not everyone is an enemy. There are plenty of friendly people. It's just a matter of finding them.

Are you prepared to help? Are you sure? The journey can be very dangerous! As with our book *Mary Jones and Her Bible*, you can enjoy the story even if you don't want to try the puzzles.

This is a simplified and abridged version of *Pilgrim's Progress – Special Edition*, containing illustrations and a mix of puzzles. The suggested reading age is up to perhaps ten. Older readers will find the same story told in much greater detail in *Pilgrim's Progress – Special Edition* on the next page.

eBook ISBN 13: 978-0-9933941-6-4

Paperback ISBN: 978-0-9525956-6-3
5.5 x 8.5 inches 174 pages £6.95
Available from major internet stores

Pilgrim's Progress
Special Edition
Chris Wright

This book for all ages is a great choice for young readers, as well as for families, Sunday school teachers, and anyone who wants to read John Bunyan's *Pilgrim's Progress* in a clear form.

All the old favourites are here: Christian, Christiana, the Wicket Gate, Interpreter, Hill Difficulty with the lions, the four sisters at the

House Beautiful, Vanity Fair, Giant Despair, Faithful and Talkative — and, of course, Greatheart. The list is almost endless.

The first part of the story is told by Christian himself, as he leaves the City of Destruction to reach the Celestial City, and becomes trapped in the Slough of Despond near the Wicket Gate. On his journey he will encounter lions, giants, and a creature called the Destroyer.

Christiana follows along later, and tells her own story in the second part. Not only does Christiana have to cope with her four young brothers, she worries about whether her clothes are good enough for meeting the King. Will she find the dangers in Vanity Fair that Christian found? Will she be caught by Giant Despair and imprisoned in Doubting Castle? What about the dragon with seven heads?

It's a dangerous journey, but Christian and Christiana both know that the King's Son is with them, helping them through the most difficult parts until they reach the Land of Beulah, and see the Celestial City on the other side of the Dark River. This is a story you will remember for ever, and it's about a journey you can make for yourself.

eBook ISBN: 978-0-9932760-8-8

Paperback ISBN: 978-0-9525956-7-0
5.5 x 8.5 inches 278 pages
Available from major internet stores

Agathos, The Rocky Island,
And Other Stories
Chris Wright

Once upon a time there were two favourite books for Sunday reading: *Parables from Nature* and *Agathos and The Rocky Island.*

These books contained short stories, usually with a hidden meaning. In this illustrated book is a selection of the very best of these stories, carefully retold to preserve the feel of the originals, coupled with ease of reading and understanding for today's readers.

Discover the king who sent his servants to trade in a foreign city. The butterfly who thought her eggs would hatch into baby butterflies, and the two boys who decided to explore the forbidden land beyond the castle boundary. The spider that kept being blown in the wind, the soldier who had to fight a dragon, the four children who had to find their way through a dark and dangerous forest. These are just six of the nine stories in this collection. Oh, and there's also one about a rocky island!

This is a book for a young person to read alone, a family or parent to read aloud, Sunday school teachers to read to the class, and even for grownups who want to dip into the fascinating stories of the past all by themselves. Can you discover the hidden meanings? You don't have to wait until Sunday before starting!

eBook ISBN: 978-0-9927642-7-2

Paperback ISBN: 978-0-9525956-8-7
5.5 x 8.5 inches 148 pages £5.95
Available from major internet stores

Zephan and the Vision
Chris Wright

An exciting story about the adventures of two angels who seem to know almost nothing – until they have a vision!

Two ordinary angels are caring for the distant Planet Eltor, and they are about to get a big shock – they are due to take a trip to Planet Earth! This is Zephan's story of the vision he is given before being allowed to travel with Talora, his companion angel, to help two young people fight against the enemy.

Arriving on Earth, they discover that everyone lives in a small castle. Some castles are strong and built in good positions, while others appear weak and open to attack. But it seems that the best-looking castles are not always the most secure.

Meet Castle Nadia and Castle Max, the two castles that Zephan and Talora have to defend. And meet the nasty creatures who have built shelters for themselves around the back of these castles. And worst of all, meet the shadow angels who live in a cave on Shadow Hill. This is a story about the forces of good and the forces of evil. Who will win the battle for Castle Nadia?

The events in this story are based very loosely on John Bunyan's allegory *The Holy War*.

E-book ISBN: 978-0-9932760-6-4

Paperback ISBN: 978-0-9525956-9-4
5.5 x 8.5 inches 216 pages
Available from major internet stores

Two of four short books of help in the Christian life by Chris Wright:

Starting Out – help for new Christians of all ages. Paperback ISBN 978-1-4839-622-0-7, eBook ISBN: 978-0-9933941-0-2

Running Through the Bible – a simple understanding of what's in the Bible – Paperback ISBN: 978-0-9927642-6-5, eBook ISBN: 978-0-9933941-3-3

So, What Is a Christian? An introduction to a personal faith. Paperback ISBN: 978-0-9927642-2-7, eBook ISBN: 978-0-9933941-2-6

Help! – Explores some problems we can encounter with our faith. Paperback ISBN 978-0-9927642-2-7, eBook ISBN: 978-0-9933941-1-9

Printed in Poland
by Amazon Fulfillment
Poland Sp. z o.o., Wrocław